CW00504889

First Edition

SHORT
TALL TALES

By Brian Lumley

COPYRIGHT PAGE

A Really Game Boy, from *Dark Terrors 2*, edited by Steve Jones and David Sutton, published by Victor Gollancz, an imprint of the Cassell Group, 1996.

A Dreamer's Tale, Phantasmagoria Magazine, Phantasmagoria Special Edition Series Issue #6, Brian Lumley Special Edition, edited by Trevor Kennedy, UK, 2022.

In Dublin's Fair City, from Dark Discoveries Magazine, January 2017 issue #37.

War of the Worlds II: Earthlings V Pondlings, The Do-It-Yourself-Carpenter, Decreation. 50 words or less. *Ghoul Warning and Other Omens...and Other Omens*, W. P. Ganley, Publisher and Necronomicon Press, 1999.

City Out of Time (Cthulhu Mythos poem) In *Fantasy Tales*, Vol. 1, No. 2, Winter 1977.

A Cry at Night In the fanzine *Midnight Fantasies*, No. (?) Pre-1977.

Warhorse, *Ghoul Warning*, Spectre Press,1982.

Inmate, *Ghoul Warning*, Spectre Press,1982.

FOREWARNING FOREWORD!

For instance: is there in any really short story such a sufficiency of text as to actually make an introduction worthwhile, when the only obviously acceptable truth of the matter is that there is not? Which being the case, to discuss or even hint at explaining why such a covert homunculus of a work must surely fail is the realization that it *really does not require an explanation*—nor even the hint of one—when the tale's telling in its fullness (or emptiness) will of course be its own introduction! Which is also true of any good—albeit bad—epigram...

CONTENTS

THE MAN IN THE DREAM

(THE THING IN THE MOONLIGHT)

by H. P. Lovecraft & Brian Lumley

Dreams? Just dream them, don't live them!

Morgan is not a literary man; in fact he cannot speak English with any degree of coherency. That is what makes me wonder about the words he wrote, though others have laughed.

He was alone the evening it happened. Suddenly an unconquerable urge to write came over him, and taking pen in hand he wrote the following:

My name is Howard Phillips. I live at 66 College Street, in Providence, Rhode Island. On November 24, 1927—for I know not even what the year may be now—I fell asleep and dreamed, since when I have been unable to awaken.

My dream began in a dank, reed-choked marsh that lay under a gray autumn sky, with a rugged cliff of lichen-crusted stone rising to the north. Impelled by some obscure quest, I ascended a rift or cleft in this beetling precipice, noting as I did so the black mouths of many fearsome burrows extending from both walls into the depths of the stony plateau.

At several points the passage was roofed over by the choking of the upper parts of the narrow fissure; these places being exceeding dark, and forbidding the perception of such burrows as may have existed there. In one such dark space I felt conscious of a singular accession of fright, as if some subtle and bodiless emanation from the abyss were engulfing my spirit;

but the blackness was too great for me to perceive the source of my alarm.

At length I emerged upon a table-land of moss-grown rock and scanty soil, lit by a faint moonlight which had replaced the expiring orb of day. Casting my eyes about, I beheld no living object; but was sensible of a very peculiar stirring far below me, amongst the whispering rushes of the pestilential swamp I had lately quitted.

After walking for some distance, I encountered the rusty tracks of a street railway, and the worm-eaten poles which still held the limp and sagging trolley wire. Following this line, I soon came upon a yellow, vestibuled car numbered 1852—of a plain, double-trucked type common from 1900 to 1910. It was untenanted, but evidently ready to start; the trolley being on the wire and the air-brake now and then throbbing beneath the floor. I boarded it and looked vainly about for the light switch— noting as I did so the absence of the controller handle, which thus implied the brief absence of the motorman. Then I sat down in one of the cross seats of the vehicle. Presently I heard a swishing in the sparse grass toward the left, and saw the dark forms of two men looming up in the moonlight. They had the regulation caps of a railway company, and I could not doubt but that they were conductor and motorman. Then one of them *sniffed* with singular sharpness, and raised his face to howl to the moon. The other dropped to all fours to run toward the car.

I leaped up at once and raced madly out of that car and across endless leagues of plateau till exhaustion forced me to stop—doing this not because the conductor had dropped on all fours, but because the face of the motorman was a mere white cone tapering to one blood-red tentacle...

I was aware that I only dreamed, but the very awareness was not pleasant.

Since that fearful night, I have prayed only for awakening— it has not come! Instead I have found myself an *inhabitant* of this terrible dream-world; that first night gave way to dawn, and I wandered aimlessly over the lonely swamp-lands. When night came, I still wandered, hoping for awakening. But suddenly I parted the weeds and saw before me the ancient railway car—and to one side a cone-faced thing lifted its head and in the streaming moonlight howled strangely!

It has been the same each day. Night takes me always to that place of horror. I have tried not moving, with the coming of nightfall, but I must walk in my slumber, for always I awaken with the thing of dread howling before me in the pale moonlight, and I turn and flee madly.

God! When will I awaken?

That is what Morgan wrote. I would to 66 College Street in Providence, but I fear what I might find there.

"...My own dreams being particularly vivid and real— to such an extent that I never know for sure whether or not I am dreaming until I wake up—I would not like to argue which world is the more vital; the waking world or the world of dream. Certainly the waking world is the more solid; but consider what science tells us about the atomic make-up of so-called solids—and what are you left with...?"
—Gerhard Schrach

It has been written of Howard Phillips that for him "there was not such thing as 'sleep' in the ordinary meaning or usage of the word; he passed directly from the waking world into an equally vivid and detailed dream-world, complete with conversations, odors, colours, and the feel of objects and taste of viands, but always with fantastic settings and adventures toward impending dooms and horrors in dreams that were seldom chaotic or jumbled, but often developed step by step like well-constructed narratives."

I cannot help but wonder if the writer of those words *fully* appreciated the validity of their content; for to me, knowing what I now know, they form an incontrovertible statement of terrible fact as pertinent now to myself as it was to Howard Phillips—an irrefutable truth which, while I am unable to understand the unnatural forces that make it so, fills me with awe and horror.

I had never met Howard Phillips in real life—but I did once

meet him, almost, in a dream. Not that I had ever been a dreamer of great horrors myself; yet the dreams I have known—and one in particular—have been detestable things that have haunted my subconscious until long after my return through the barrier of sleep to the comparative safety of the waking world. I wish now that I was never drawn to read any of Howard Phillips' work, that I never had indulged the strange need to collect those laboriously detailed nightmares he termed "stories."

Just when it was I recognized the dark affinity between Phillips and myself I cannot say. Certainly his tales fascinated me, binding me in those *outré* yet absolutely authentic spells of which he was undoubtedly the master-weaver, but it was not until I read *The Thing in the Moonlight* that I really became aware of something out of the ordinary. From the moment I started to read it, from the opening description of the reed-choked marsh beneath grey autumn skies to the advent of the cone-faced things in the motormen's caps, I fell completely under the spell of the story—so that I came to know it intimately, almost as if I had written it myself.

It gradually dawned on me that this was much more than just another story. I recognized the very feel of the words and the texture of the mood. I actually *knew* the cleft in the beetling precipice which Howard Phillips had climbed in his dream. I had seen the mouths of the burrows which he described extending into the depths of the stony plateau to which he had ascended. I had known, as had he, those exceedingly dark places wherein dwelt subtle and bodiless emanations from the abyss; but I did not remember ever fearing them. And I, too, in some remote and all but forgotten existence, had cast my eyes over that tableland of moss-grown rock and scanty soil lit by faint moonlight. I dimly *remembered* those rusty, unused tracks of the street railway and the worm-eaten poles straining to hold aloft their limp and sagging burden of rotting trolley wire; and also the yellow double-trucked, vestibuled trolley-car—it, too, was part of that inexplicably familiar dream world.

And so I suppose that it was only natural the thing should come to me one night...

No sooner had I laid my tired head upon the pillow than

I was there—I was in that region of lonely swamp-lands, streaming moonlight and weeds. Oh! It was real—so real that I did not even remember going to bed, I knew nothing whatever of my waking life. I had *always* been in that land; I was part of it.

Nor was I alone. I did not look at my companion, for I had seen him often before and knew him well. We had a job to do and were on our way to do it. Behind us friendly burrowers gaped in the darkness of beetling crag-cast shadows as we crossed the weird, yet well-known and convivial terrain of long grasses and weeds.

After walking for some distance in silence we encountered the familiar rusty tracks of the street railway, and following these we soon came upon the yellow, vestibuled car—number 1852—which of course I had know would be there and waiting. But as we made our way through the grass to the left of the car, I noticed something in the air—a presence in conflict with the norm of the place.

In that instant, as I suddenly remembered the real waking world, I gasped aloud...and was horrified that my gasp, rather than being an involuntary exhalation, came to my ears as a monstrously altered animal grunt or sniff. Then, in the flooding moonlight, I glanced up at the car and saw a man...

Not just *any* man. For this was no stranger sitting there but Howard Phillips. Howard Phillips dreaming his dream, and I was in that dream, *and he sat there staring at me in horror!*

I knew him at once and shouted his name in awe and bewilderment. But it was not a shouted name that echoed back to me—rather was it the cry of a beast! And suddenly I knew. I knew that *I* was the thing in the moonlight, and as Phillips fled from his seat I turned to see my silent companion drop to all fours and hurl himself in the direction of the car.

In awful, stunned disbelief, I put my hand—my paw—up to my face and felt that...that...

Mercifully, I awoke.

A dream? Only a nightmare brought on by too much reading

and too vivid an imagination? Perhaps. Yet now, while others lie drowning in dreams, I am left to toss and turn upon my bed, clawing desperately at the wall of sleep, afraid to close my eyes in the terrifying knowledge that the world which lies just across the dark threshold of dream is real!

As real as the crumpled and mildewed motorman's cap I found on waking beside my tumbled, sweat-soaked bet...!

LATE SHOPPING

Aliens and other monsters don't always arrive in spaceships.

Dreaming …

It was evening and I was out walking through the town, exploring a street I had never used before … which was strange in itself for I knew the town rather well. There were one or two people about, late shoppers, though most of the stores were already closed. One supermarket was open, however, its lights seeming to beckon. People were entering, milling about inside behind the plate-glass windows, coming out with packages and parcels and disappearing into the grey light of evening. It would soon be dark.

"They're still doing business," said a young woman beside me. "Must be a closing-down sale."

"Or they have a promotion on," I answered. "Booze and cigarettes at pre-budget prices, maybe."

She smiled at me. Her lips and cheeks were very red, eyes and hair bright in the glow from the windows. She turned away. The pneumatic doors hissed open and swallowed her up. Seen through the glass of the doors she looked different somehow and seemed to move awkwardly.

What was the store's big attraction? I wondered. Anyway, I needed cigarettes. The pneumatic doors obliged as I approached, allowing me to step through them into—

Darkness!

Someone had switched off the lights just as I entered. But where were all the people? And why was it so pitch black? I felt my guts tighten. There was no street outside the windows.

There were no windows. There was just the darkness...

Somebody gasped.

I felt my hairs stiffen at the back of my neck as I spun on my heel. Maybe a dozen paces away the young woman who had smiled at me stood looking up at a high, blinking red light above a metal grill shaped something like a frowning mouth. A mechanical voice began to repeat over and over, "Just stand still and keep looking at the light. Everything is fine. Just stand still and keep looking at the light. Everything is fine."

She stood as if frozen, her face turned up to the light. Her eyes were staring, her young face glowing red and disappearing in time with the light's blinking. Red, and gone—red, and gone—red, and gone, gone, gone!

Gone...

She was no longer there.

The floor lurched beneath my feet, a conveyor belt that carried me toward the red light. I stepped backward but the floor moved faster. In another moment the light was above me and the floor jerked to a halt.

The mechanical voice said, "Just stand still and keep looking at the—" but I wasn't listening. Neither was I looking, nor was I standing still. Not for long.

I *had* looked at the light—just once, the merest glimpse—before I snatched my eyes away and leapt into the darkness. The light had looked like a huge, blood-shot, hypnotically blinking eye!

The floor came alive again, more urgently this time, throbbing under my feet like some great black heart. I felt myself hurried along, stumbled, fell, rolled and came up against a wall. The mechanical voice was harsher now and more demanding:

"Stand still! Look at the light!"

I scrambled to my feet, clutched at the wall and felt a crack in the otherwise smooth surface. I hung onto the crack and trotted to counter the movement of the floor. The floor speeded up; the mechanical voice, too. "Stand still! Look at the light. The light. The light..."

I ran, my heart beginning to pound. I clawed at the wall,

dug my straining fingers into the crack, put all my weight and ebbing energy into the effort.

The wall cracked open with a pneumatic hiss, sending me staggering into the street. The street was almost deserted now and no one noticed me panting, sobbing, standing in the doorway and leaning against the wall. As I straightened up the doors hissed open again, ejecting the young woman. Behind her the supermarket was—well, a supermarket! It too, was almost empty. A few more people came out. I stood watching them, gawping, disbelieving. What the hell had happened to me in there?

At last the place was empty. The lights dimmed and went out. I was alone in the street.

The glass doors gave a last *hiss* and opened a fraction. The huge red bloodshot eye stared out at me and the doors slowly, almost calculatingly, closed upon it. I turned to run and bumped into the young woman. I didn't know why she was still standing there. But her eyes were dull. The lustre had gone out of her hair, her face. She was drab.

She smiled, but vacantly, and I thought I saw a trickle of saliva at the corner of her mouth. She carried a paper bag that dripped red onto the pavement, and somehow I knew that the bag contained her soul, ripped out of her.

I stumbled around her and ran, not looking back. And soon after that I woke up...

I was in town a few days later and like a fool went looking for the supermarket. I couldn't even find the street! But—

There seemed to be an awful lot of vacant, pallid-looking people on the bus, and the town itself was full of them. Then again, there were lots of slugs in the garden, too. Things always look worse when it's raining ...

NOTE: 'Late Shopping' was inspired by one of the author's darkest dreams.

SPIDER IN THE BATH

Well, you could always use the shower, okay?

L ast night I had a nightmare, and boy was I in trouble.
    It started nice and easy. Don't they all? Myself, I've always found that the most nightmarish nightmares are the repetitious ones. The ones where your feet seem stuck in treacle, where there's no escape no matter what you do. When try as you might the horror keeps finding you. A theme repeated endlessly, like a Möbius strip. Even something comparatively innocuous, repeated often enough can become a nightmare.

That's what it was like. And yet it had novelty too.

The nightmare started with me waking up. That is to say, I dreamed it was morning. I got up, stumbled about a bit like I always do, put on the immersion heater for my morning bath. Then I went to brush my teeth—and found a spider in the bath.

He was, oh, half an inch long?—the hairy variety. And red-eyed. In the gloom of the bathroom, with the curtains still drawn, I could see the tiny glow of his faceted eyes—and they seemed to be looking at me. Shuddering, I flushed him away. *Ugh!*

After coffee I went to the loo. Sitting there, half-through a yawn, I saw he was back. No, this must be his brother. Bigger, hairier. Scarier! All of an inch long at least. Patterned on his fat back like a skull. I had known there were moths like that, but spiders?

When I flushed him away, the grid almost refused his bulk. His legs hung on like grim death long after his body had sagged under the rush of water. But at last, leg-by-leg, he submitted and was gone in a burp and a gurgle. God, I *hate* spiders!

Later, out of curiosity, I looked in again.

God *damn!* He was there—or his uncle! Two inches long or more, slowly, laboriously climbing the bath's porcelain cliff. I had to use the handle of my toothbrush to force him down the plughole. Tight squeeze, too. *I bet that hurt, you big hairy bastard!* And this time after washing him away I put in the plug.

Then—more coffee, and toast and honey—the water getting hot now—and me humming to myself as I piled my robe and slippers on the chair beside the bathroom door. And my humming dying in my nose, turning to a snort as I glanced in and saw that the plug was out.

Now I could have sworn I'd left the plug in…

I suppose it was then that I knew this was a dream, recognizing it as the sort that rapidly becomes a nightmare. It happens every time I have a large supper.

Frowning, I stuck my head round the door. Nothing in the bath. I looked in the sink, the loo. No spider. But…under the shiny steel grid in the bath's plughole, something black and hairy blinked and glared. Red-faceted eyes seemed to shutter themselves as I peered closer. Down there, nothing but darkness.

I turned on the cold tap and gave the plughole a quick burst anyway, just to be on the safe side. Then I opened the curtains, looked again.

Nothing. My imagination.

I began to hum again, put in the plug, reached for my bath salts. Oh-oh! Not there. Must have put them in the bedroom.

I draped my towel over the bath's rim, went to get the salts, returned with them to the bathroom—and stopped dead in my tracks. The plug was out again, and the shiny steel lattice of the grill had been snipped and pushed upwards and outwards.

And in the bath, under the hem of my towel where I'd draped it, *something moved!* The tip of a hooked, hairy leg, thick as a pencil, nervously vibrated where it projected.

I snatched up the towel, backed away from the monster my action revealed. He was the daddy of all creepy-crawlies! Six or seven inches of glowering hideousness! But still—thank God!—incapable of escaping from the bath. When finally he did get a leg up over the rim, I smacked at it flat-handed and knocked it free. Blood immediately smeared my palm where it had contacted the spider's chitin. He was razor-sharp!

I backed out, fetched a long-handled screwdriver, nerved myself and sidled up to the bath. There he was—nine or ten inches of him now—but he had his back to me. It was now or never. I jabbed hard.

The screwdriver slid over armoured scales, slipped between them, went in. And in another moment he was going crazy on the tool's blade, leaking yellow goo and screaming. Screaming, yes! High-pitched, shrill, more a shivering hiss than a scream proper. Like when live lobsters go into the pot.

I snatched the window open, lobbed him out and down with a jerk of my arm, so that he slid off the point of the screwdriver into empty air...and was gone.

He left a thread of stinking goo on the windowsill. The screwdriver was covered in the same stuff. I slammed the window shut, tossed the screwdriver into the sink and scalded it with hot water. And now the nightmare started to take over in earnest.

I mean, you'd think by now I'd lost all interest in bathing, wouldn't you? But isn't that just the nature of a nightmare? Repetition, see.

I took the screwdriver back to my tool cupboard, brought back a pair of pliers, which I used to force the broken spokes of the grid down into the plughole. Then, when I could once more get the plug properly seated, I turned on both taps and liberally sprinkled in bath salts. The bathroom quickly filled with lavender-scented steam.

I tested the water...*ow!* Hot! But bearable. I got in, started to lie back, noticed that the window was open...

Open?

Open!

Something sticky and yellow dripped on me.

The bastard was on the ceiling—eighteen inches of hairy, leggy horror!

I flopped about on my back in the hot water...couldn't find purchase...banged my head...stared transfixed up at him. And him at me, but the terror was all mine. I mean, what the hell did *he* have to be scared of? Nothing! Not with those great curved salivating fangs gnashing in his awful face!

And then…then he dropped on me!

I woke up gibbering, shrieking, heart banging away fit to come right through my ribs. And my legs were like rubber. I bounced off every wall on my way to the loo. But I didn't get to go.

I couldn't go, and I *won't* go.

See, there's a tiny spider in the bath—the hairy variety, with a pattern like a skull on his back—and boy, am I in trouble!

MEMORY?

Just as well we can't see it both ways.

"Memory," yes. If that's the right word for it. Fine if one is recalling the past as one experienced it. For then, of course, memory *is* the right, indeed the only, word.

But as for myself: well, I remember the past, the present, and the future; *my* past, present, and future, that is…which gives me pause when I consider the word "memory."

Maybe it's some kind of kink in my genes, my DNA. Some kind of mutation? I mean, if it was only the dim and distant past I remembered, I might try to explain it away as *ancestral* memory; which if it exists at all is surely more instinct than actual memory. The moorhen chick doesn't *remember* how to swim when it leaves its shattered shell and plunges straight into the water; no, it's simply a matter of instinct.

Ah, but *my* memories are real, detailed, and coloured! And it's not just one past I remember, but many. I don't remember whole lives, it should be understood, mainly snatches of them. There wouldn't be enough room in my brain for complete files of all the lives I've lived! So when I say I remember my past, in fact I mean my *pasts*—plural, yes—and likewise my futures.

As for the present me: he's only one of many who have been or will be…

Anyway, I've tried to figure it out, considered it from all angles, not least the scientific. Wasn't it Albert Einstein who said, "Yesterday, today, and tomorrow," (time, in fact) "is an illusion—albeit a persistent one."? He said something of the sort, anyway.

So maybe he was like me. If he could remember his futures… well, mightn't that explain his genius: that he *remembered* the ideas of some future Einsteinian descendant or reincarnation?

And there's another word: "reincarnation," which has to be considered the other side of the coin. For the notion is definitely *un*scientific: the idea of me living again, and again, and again, retaining or remembering bits of what went before…but not of what's still to come, surely? Ah, there's the rub!

Or perhaps the current me, the one I *think* I am, is only a memory of me as remembered by some far future me! (And here a thought: some of my far future me, well, recently they've been lasting far too long: greater than mere memories, it was as if I was actually living them!)

But as for the past, I admit to being confused…for how can one possibly remember being a being that *couldn't* possibly have had any sort of memory to speak of? What weird temporal, telepathic linkage could there be between a mind like that (if "mind" is the right word for it) and a mind like mine? For you see, I can remember being a myxomycete—a slime mould—on a rotting log in what was presumably a prehistoric forest. No, I didn't know what I was at the time, of course not, only that I was, and then not with any degree of certainty.

And I remember what I think must have been the Devonian, where as a sea slug I shrank from carnivorous starfish. Later I was a Thecodont, and later still a monkey. And please don't try to deny me my lineage, for according to the Double Helixes of Being even the mighty oak is my cousin, however far removed.

As for men: I was of an obscure branch of Australopithecus and hunted elephants in what might just have been Suffolk. How can I know that? But how do I know *any* of this? And then I was Ung, Chief of the Unga, a tribe of *Home erectus*. We too hunted our food… we cooked our meat while warming ourselves by the fire. And it seems like only yesterday that I was Jeremy Hoyle, an engineer proud to be working under the great Isambard Kingdom Brunel toward the completion of his Avon Gorge suspension bridge. But that last is more recently in the past, of course, (1863 to be exact), while presently I'm simply myself.

And despite that they may try to tell you I am not, I can assure you that I *am* most definitely myself...

But as for tomorrow and tomorrow:

Ah! soon I'll be Jason G. Adams, on a great launch platform orbiting Luna. And beyond that I'll be the billionaire owner of a diamond-mining concern in the asteroid belt, though I my-then-self will never leave my grand palace on the island of Crete. And three hundred years from now I'll be Mustapha Haqur, proud member of the hundred-member crew of the first vessel to cross interstellar space and land on an Earth-like world a thousand light-years away.

Very wonderful things, all. Ah, but not all future things are wonderful! For I am the one—the great scientist, Gordon Elvis Bennet—who will alert a world at war of a rogue meteorite as black as the Devil's backside that will come roaring out of the sun sight unseen with such destructive power as to put Man's measly weapons to shame! Only ask the dinosaurs...

But as now, so in that future time of Gordon Elvis Bennet; they won't listen, won't believe. And then the mighty thunders, the lava rains, and the destruction of Mankind. But didn't God tell us that He would do it by fire next time?

Huh! They didn't listen to Him, either.

And so "The End," but not the very end, not yet awhile. For in a mainly dead world, down in the deeps, a future me shall be a scurry of life on the rim of a great black smoker, a shrimpy sort of thing feeding on the even smaller feeders on vile chemical soups ejected from the abyss. And I shall be him for quite some time—far too long for my liking...

But there, enough is enough and I won't go on. These memories of mine get longer with each visit, and I foresee the approach of a time when I shall be a slime mould again—perhaps permanently. That is something I dare not contemplate.

And anyway it's almost teatime, when I shall complain that my room is far too small; also that the padding in the walls is tasteless and completely indigestible...

THE LECTURE

Kids? Who would be a teacher, eh?

The old professor was nearing the end of his lecture now, and with all his years of experience he had it timed to perfection. Glancing at his timepiece, he gave a low grunt of satisfaction; the bell was due at any moment now, and then this lot would go on to their next classroom, their next period of instruction.

It wasn't just an immaculate sense of timing, however, that gave the professor his warm glow of satisfaction; but this time he felt he'd actually managed to impart a degree of knowledge—felt that this motley band of students had got something out of it—which in this day and age was an accomplishment in itself. For him and them both!

But then again his subject, "prehistoric mass extinctions," had been especially fascinating. Of course, the professor would consider it so—as would he consider almost any facet of life in the ancient world—because he was a paleontologist. But as for his class...ordinarily, the only rocks he might expect to excite *their* interest wouldn't be fossils. Rocks as in rock-'n-roll, yes—or maybe (though heaven forbid) rocks as in certain dreadful mind-destroying drugs—and quite definitely rocks as in "getting them off." Oh yes! Sex, drugs, and rock-'n-roll. It had always been so, and he wasn't so old that he'd forgotten...

Ah, but this time the professor had chosen a subject that was irresistible—one that he considered the single infallible spear-point in his entire paleontological arsenal—the subject that was guaranteed to penetrate even that seething mental smog known to obscure every young adult's hormone- and/or pheromone-driven mind.

As for why this was so, perhaps it was terror: the thought that it could, might, and probably would happen again. An even bigger mass extinction which nothing would survive—including them. After all, there were plenty of asteroids out there even now; not to mention colossal swarms of comets, those so-called "dirty snowballs" that were so very much harder than snow. And all of this free-floating stony debris being lured by the sun, drawn in from far beyond the solar system's rim.

Or perhaps it was simply the "natural" hypnotic attraction (well, to the young and immature) of the invisible threat: the possibility, however remote, of planetary catastrophe, felt in their inner beings as the tremblings of adventurous expectancy, the thrill of a challenge yet to be faced. Ah, for when one is young life is forever! But when one is old…

The professor blinked and brought his meandering mind back to the present, for it was now time to finish up.

"So there you have it," he said, glancing from face to rapt face. "The fossil record cannot be denied; we know it happened, and more than once, but still we can't be sure—not absolutely sure—exactly *how* it happened. And while the controversy rages on, I believe it degrades the science of paleontology that such mass extinction theories as are propounded today range from the sublime to the ridiculous. Having said that, however, it is my intention to make such theories the subject of my next lecture. Which is why, before closing, I'll merely skim over them.

"The two most likely theories involve, one: the collision of our world with huge space rocks, which is to say meteors or comets, slamming into the Earth at unthinkable velocities; and two: extensive volcanic activity releasing vast lava flows and clouds of poisonous gases. Better still—or perhaps worse—you might want to consider a combination of the two: first, the hugely destructive collision, causing atmospheric depletion and fearful earthquakes, followed at once by vast floods of molten rock erupting through the planet's shattered crust. That would be my personal preference.

"As for some of those rather more fanciful theories that I

mentioned…well, I did warn you that several were ridiculous. For example:

"The planet was overpopulated, infested by so many diverse species that they virtually farted themselves to death, killed off by their own methane emissions!" (As usual the professor's unanticipated ribaldry sufficed to produce a stamping of feet, broad grins right across the class, and snorts of scatological amusement…all of which encouraged him to draw a deep breath and continue.)

"Or how about this:

"In the future—in a period when we're being eaten out of house and planet by lesser species—we'll invent time travel and journey into the past to murder them in their evolutionary infancy, thus ensuring our presence today." (More chuckles and snorting and stamping of feet.)

"And finally, silliest of all, there's this one:

"Converging parallel universes—if you believe in such— glance off each other, and in the ensuing chaos all life except the hardiest of land creatures, certain aquatic worms, and the deep-sea crustacea which thrive around black smokers are wiped out *en masse*. Which tends to make us—or rather you, since I exclude myself—the descendants of primitive burrowers, or of rock-boring worms, or of…shrimps? Well, personally speaking, and judging by this class, I'd be inclined to accept the latter before the former. For while I cannot admit of parallel worlds, just a single glance at certain members of my current audience would seem to me to offer abundant proof of severe *degenerative* as opposed to the usual evolutionary processes!

"But of course—" The professor raised his voice against a rising gale of laughter, "—of course, we must first believe in parallel universes. Including, one must assume, those where our species were the unfortunate victims of these extinctions…"

That quietened them a little, and in the momentary lull the professor glanced again at his timepiece. Ah! Dead on time!

And proving it conclusively, the bell sounded.

"Leave the room just as you found it—in good order!" The old professor's rasping, vibrating voice rang out again.

But rising from their great stone benches, crowding noisily

through the towering arched exit from the massive lecture hall, the students were already leaving.

Such a thunderous stampede!

As usual the pack of raptor youths led the exodus, while a female triceratops brought up the rear. Not so much because she was slow, but mainly because she waited shyly to lay the fresh, juicy branch of a flowering tree fern on the professor's marble lectern...

HELL IS A PERSONAL PLACE

But then again, how's your personality?

The uniformed man in the bunker gave a last stiff-armed salute—or it should have been but most of the stiffness had disappeared now, and his uniform with its black leather cross-strap was less than crisp; indeed it was dusty with a fine layer of the concrete powder which kept drifting down from the low ceiling as the thudding concussions crept closer and closer—then put the muzzle of his pistol to his head. With feeble cries of *Heil Hitler* ringing in his ears from those whose pale, sickly faces surrounded him—cries *so* feeble and faces *so* sickly he felt he really should shoot these knock-kneed imbeciles first, or even instead; except that would mean being alone, and maybe not enough ammunition left to finish the job—he pulled the trigger.

It was so simple it was great, he thought. Even glorious!

At the last moment he had closed his eyes. Small in stature but hardly insignificant, *not now, anyway,* with his hair parted in its distinctive style, *which so bloody many enemies of the Reich found so bloody funny!,* he reeled from the expected devastation of his brain as the hammer bullet fell on his grape head…

…And reeled again as the realization dawned that he'd felt nothing!

"What?" he cried in astonishment, and then rage: "*What!* What, what, WHAT? A gun that doesn't work? But should I be surprised? Of course not! Why should I be surprised? My army didn't work, my navy didn't work, my air force *certainly* didn't work, so why should one small pistol? Am I the only one in the entire bloody *Vaterland* who *has* bloody worked?"

He turned to hurl the offending weapon in the nearest sickly face, only to discover that his hand was empty and that the nearest face had no flesh, sickly or otherwise.

A tall, thin figure in black sat on a flat-topped rock and gazed at him through empty orbs from beneath the peaked cowl of his robe. At his feet there lay a rusting, neglected scythe and a bone-dry whetstone.

"What?" said Hitler. "What?"

"I didn't say anything," said the man in black. He shuffled his sandaled feet a little, and the knuckles of his toes gleamed bone-white through a lattice of ancient leather.

"Explain!" Hitler cried, advancing a short, sharp pace. But then he paused, looked beyond the somber figure seated on the rock, gazed upon three distinct arcs of a distant horizon. One arc lay in a dark blue, near-impenetrable shadow.

"Limbo," said the skeletal man in black. "For those who are blameless but desire only rest—an eternity of rest."

Hitler's eyes went to the next arc of the horizon, where golden rays lanced skywards into azure heavens from the gleaming minarets and domes of a city unthinkably beautiful. And the cowled figure explained: "Reward—for those who have loved and aspired to even greater love, and who now in their turn are loved."

Finally there remained only the third arc. Red and yellow fires leaped there, and a faint wind brought a sulphur reek, mixed with which Hitler believed he could hear, very distantly, tumultuous cries of torture and terror. It seemed a familiar sort of place, and the man in black offered no explanation but merely gloomed on Hitler from the deep, dark sockets of his eyes. He stood up, and Hitler saw how tall and thin he was. But of course, he would be.

"So you are Death," the little man mused. "Strange, I never really believed in you—not for myself.

"But for many, *many* others," Death answered. "So many, indeed, that I was beginning to think you'd be the last of all. Why, you're a legend!"

Hitler preened a little. "I am?" Then he frowned. "But of course I am! I know that!"

"You very nearly did me out of my job," Death went on. "They came so thick and fast I couldn't keep up! See my scythe there, all rusted where once it gleamed silver? Ah, well, and now I'll have to get it bright again. But yes, you are a legend. So was Atilla, and the Asian wizard who first created the Black Death and sent it scurrying westward, and Cain, who was the greatest murderer of them all."

"Cain?" Hitler wrinkled his brow. Who was this upstart Cain?

"With a single stroke, he killed one fourth of the world's population," Death explained, as if he'd read the little dictator's thoughts. "Even you haven't managed that!"

Hitler struck a pose, peered at the three different arcs of horizon. "That was never my intention," he said (Death's wit escaping him entirely). "I intended only the elimination of certain—or several—ethnic groups. *Large* ethnic groups, true, but—" And he paused, then scowled, then looked amazed as he took a first involuntary step toward the arc of smoldering fire and sulphur stench. Involuntary, yes—invoked by the will of some Other.

"Your time's up," Death explained.

Hitler looked again at the three distinct horizons, keeping till last that direction in which he felt compelled. The way to Limbo was a broad swath of deep green grass, blown languidly in a cool, pleasantly-scented breeze. The way to Just Reward was paved with blue crystal tiles of infinite delicacy, where fountains played every now and then, and strange, delicious-seeming fruit grew on low golden bushes by the roadside. Alas, the path to Hell was parched, where the earth was cracked open and scarred like scrubland in a drought.

The ex-dictator fought against the next step, leaned back against its pull, to no avail. His jackboot came up, moved forward and plumped down, pointing him unmistakably along the desiccated track. He stumbled, half-turned, said: "Wait! I have not interrogated—I mean questioned—I mean you have not *told* me the things I need to…"

"There is nothing else," Death was brief. "The rest lies in the hands of *der Führer.*"

"*Der Fü—?*" Hitler was astonished, outraged—his blood boiled! He would have stamped his foot, but when he lifted it, it took another involuntary pace toward Hell. "Is that what he calls himself, this … this *devil?*"

Death came pacing after, loping like a long shadow to overtake Hitler's every-quickening march. "Hell is a personal place," he said, "and Satan has many forms. One for every damned soul. For yours he is *der Führer.*"

Hitler paled a very little. "What's he like, this Satan?"

"Very handsome," Death shrugged, walking alongside the new arrival. "And not a little conceited. Alas, that was always his trouble. Oh!—and of course he's *not* an Aryan…"

"Not an Aryan?" Hitler repeated him, dazedly. Then his eyes suddenly brightened into feverish intensity. "Not an Aryan!" His nostrils flared. "Hah!" he gave a stiff-armed salute. "Then it's time there were some *changes* around here! Big changes!"

Death chuckled, however humourlessly. "But aren't you a rather small man, Adolf," he said, "to be dreaming of such sweeping changes? After all, *he* is very big."

"I was small once before," Hitler snapped. "But a man's destiny is fashioned by his dreams, not by his stature."

"That might well be true," Death answered, "but where you're going Satan fashions the dreams. All of them. And each and every one, a nightmare! And before I forget—" he produced a black patch in the shape of a six-pointed star and quickly slapped it on Hitler's left breast just under the cross-strap. The star at once seared through jacket and shirt, burning itself into flesh.

Hitler yelped, tore open his smoking jacket and shirt, then tucked in his quivering chin and stared down in horror at the star which was now part of him, like a great black birthmark or some hideous melanoma, made that much more hideous by what it conveyed.

"Preposterous!" he sputtered then through tears of pain and rage. "I am not a Jew!"

"And I repeat," said Death, enigmatically, "that Satan is not an Aryan. But in Hell, each has his role to play."

Hitler's shoulders slumped, but his jackboots kept marching. The fiery horizon was that much closer now; heat came gusting in scorching waves, carrying the worst possible stenches; the cries of tortured millions were loud and growing louder.

"*Verdammt!*" Hitler's frustration overflowed. "Where is my Third Reich now?" Tears, apparently of anguish, flowed down his face.

"Gone," Death answered his question, "but the Fourth lies directly ahead. Except it is not yours. *Vorwärts!*"

Then the Grim Reaper came to a halt, and watched as Hitler went striding off toward his ultimate solution. The ex-dictator glanced back once, fearfully, at Death, but already the gaunt figure of that timeless being had been left far behind. Hitler sighed his resignation and faced front.

In the near distance, curling over the balefires, a huge black swastika was blazoned on the sprawl of a vast scarlet flag...

PROBLEM CHILD

And you think pubic hair's an itchy bitch!

My symptoms, Dr. Trent said, were those of developing schizophrenia, split personality, but I could "counter such tendencies by recording details of them diary-wise, or by talking to yourself about them, thus recognizing and resolving the peculiarities of your dualism when controlled by your more 'normal' archetype." Ye Gods! Do they all talk like that, I wonder? Still, he sounded like he knew what he was talking about, and so—

Since my hands weren't much for writing, I started to talk to myself. And you know, his idea was all right in a way; that is, chatting to myself about it did seem to help—initially. But now, well, I don't see old Trent anymore, I haven't for a long, long time.

Wonder how he's getting on. Trent the quack—the so-called "psychiatrist"—the head-shrinker. I should never have taken my problem to him in the first place.

My "problem!"

I suspect that old Trent was laughing at me really, that he never did believe me. Even then, though, I could have proved the things I told him...if I had really wanted to. I could have cut my nails for him—and then stayed around while they grew again!

"Six times a day?" I remember him asking. "You cut your nails six times *a day?* Well, they look perfectly normal nails to me!"

And it was true, they were perfectly normal nails—to look

at! But they simply grew too fast. They still do; in fact the speed at which they grow has increased! Until recently I was cutting them up to eight times daily. Now I just don't bother. And I remember how, if I slept for more than three hours at a stretch...

It's murder to wake up and find your nails long and black—and hooked!

And I used to worry about getting jackets to fit my hump; but knowing what I know now—well, who needs jackets?

My hump: I remember when I was a kid, just a little kid, how my friends used to say I had a small hump. Now I have a big hump. I once went for treatment for curvature of the spine... Hah! There's a laugh. "Curvature of the spine," indeed! It made life hell at the orphanage, though.

Of course in those days I didn't have my fingernail-toenail thing. That didn't start until I was out of my teens, till after I left the orphanage, and even then the growth rate wasn't much in the beginning. Like the hair. I remember when I first started to shave my chin. What's more, I remember when I started shaving my body!

You should try to imagine the difficulty living when you can't go out in public for more than two or three house at a stretch. Life was *not* easy. In the end I got a job as a night watchman...

By then I had given up shaving my chest, arms, and legs; I simply concentrated on my face. This was so that I could sit by my night watchman's brazier in those hours when the last drunks are going home without attracting too much attention. In the quieter hours of the night I would shave again, as often as I needed it, and I'd also cut my nails, which had been bothering me for some time by then.

It's really surprising how many night watchmen have humps...

I lived in a boardinghouse. A sleazy place moldering on the outskirts of the city. I had a room on the ground floor, and I could sneak out unnoticed when I wanted to. Not that that was very often; rarely during daylight. It was all too much. All that shaving and cutting...and creaming.

Creaming! Have I mentioned my skin? No, I haven't

mentioned my skin. Well, that didn't begin until after all my other little blemishes were well established. My skin started to rough over.

Rough over!—regular ichthyosis, it was—like psoriasis gone rampant, with knobs on! I had to cream the skin on my face before I could do anything or go anywhere. I used a skin-colored cream, a "woman's preparation," which did the job pretty well. Makes you wonder, though, what lurks beneath the surface of some of those dolly faces in the girlie magazines, doesn't it?

Of course, in the early days, I saw a doctor about it (a *real* doctor, as opposed to old Trent) but he could do nothing—except fill useless prescriptions. After a few visits he wouldn't even see me. I don't think he liked my bad breath.

The whole thing reached a head some six months back when I started to go off my food. Up until then I could fancy almost anything—eggs, fish, beans—anything I could cook up for myself or get out of a can. It started when I got sick every time I ate something. Soon it had reached the stage where I would open a can and gag at the very smell of the contents, no matter what. I remember leaving a can of chopped steak lying around open and untouched for over a week. I was living on bread and water by then, but even so I was still sick sometimes. On the ninth day I ate the steak straight out of the can. I wasn't sick! I ate stinking, rotten steak for a long time before it dawned on me to come and live here. By then it had also dawned on me what was "wrong" with me!

It's simply this: there's *nothing* wrong with me!

I mean, just think about it: hands spade-shaped and hard as hell, for digging; a mouth (have I mentioned my mouth?) like a sucker, for slurping up soft stuff; big square teeth—I've *always* had them—for grinding hard stuff; flaky, blotched skin and black tufts of coarse hair all over my body, matching up perfectly with the shadows and mottled background on my natural habitat...

Yes, *natural*—for me!

I remember (it seems like years ago) a record by someone who used to sing Country and Western songs. It was about a boy named Sue, and how that boy hunted down his father for giving him a girl's name. I, too, will hunt down my father. One night I'll leave this place and hunt him down. I'll find him, and there and then I'll kill him with my claw hands and suck him up with my sucker mouth, and grind him with my strong, square teeth.

My mother, too.

Oh, they didn't call me Sue. They didn't call me anything, just left me on the doorstep of the orphanage. Was I so abnormal? Did I look so—freakish? They could have hid me, brought me along until I fitted in with them. Or perhaps there were others with them who wouldn't allow it, who feared that my presence (I imagine I made a pretty human-looking baby) might attract the attention of ...people.

They couldn't afford that, I suppose. After all, it's only recently, so to speak, that people have stopped believing in my kind. My race has all but died out in the minds of men; like fairies and vampires and werewolves—but *I* know we're real!

Yes, one night I'll go away from here and make my way in the shadows to another place. It'll need to be soon for there's no food here now. Perhaps I'll pick up a couple of the night watchmen on the way! And when we've cleaned the next place out, then we'll move on again. And one night I'll find my father.

Oh!—I'll find him, all right. One night, sooner or later, I'll find him...

After all, there aren't that many graveyards...

THE SORCERER'S DREAM

*As translated by Thelred Gustau…from Teh Atht's
Legends of the Olden Runes.*

Seems no one warned him about dreams…

I, The Atht, have dreamed a dream; and now, before dawn's
light may steal it from my old mind—while yet Gleeth the
blind God of the Moon rides the skies over Klühn and the stars
of night peep and leer hideously—I write it down in the pages
of my rune-book, wherein all the olden runes are as legends
unfolded. For I have pondered the great mysteries of time
and space, have solved certain of the riddles of the Ancients
Themselves, and all such knowledge is writ in my rune-book
for the fathoming of sorcerers as yet unborn.

As to why I dreamed this dream, plumbing the Great Abyss
of future time to the very END itself, where only the gaunt
black Tomb of the Universe gapes wide and empty, my reasons
were many. They were born in mummy-dust sifted down to me
through the centuries; in the writings of mages ancient when
the world was still young; in cipherless hieroglyphs graven
in the stone of Geph's broken columns; aye, and in the vilest
nightmares of shrieking madmen, whose visions had driven
them mad. And such as these reasons were they drew me as the
morning sun draws up the ocean mists on Theem'hdra's bright
strand, for I cannot suffer a mystery to go unfathomed.

The mystery was this: that oft and again over the years I had
heard whispers of a monstrous alien God who seeped down
from the stars when the world was an inchoate infant—whose

name, Cthulhu, was clouded with timeless legends and obscured in half-forgotten myths and nameless lore—and such whispers as I had heard troubled me greatly...

Concerning this Cthulhu a colleague in olden Chlangi, the warlock Nathor Tarqu, had been to the temple of the Elder Ones in Ulthar in the land of Earth's dreams to consult the Pnakotic Manuscript; and following that visit to Ulthar he had practised exceedingly strange magicks before vanishing forever from the known world of men. Since that time Chlangi has become a fallen city, and close by in the Desert of Sheb the Lamia Orbiquita has builded her castle, so that now all men fear the region and call Chlangi the Shunned City.

I, too, have been to Ulthar, and I count it a blessing that on waking I could not recall what I read in the Pnakotic Manuscript—only such awful names as were writ therein, such as Cthulhu, Tsathoggua, and Ubbo-Sathla. And there was also mention of one Ghatanothoa, a son of Cthulhu to whom a dark temple even now towers in Theem'hdra, in a place that I shall not name. For I know the place is doomed, that there is a curse upon the temple and its priests, and that when they are no more their names shall be stricken from all records...

Even so, and for all this, I would never have entertained so long and unhealthy an interest in loathly Lord Cthulhu had I not myself heard His call in uneasy slumbers; that call which turns men's minds, beckoning them on to vile worship and viler deeds. Such dreams visited themselves upon me after I had spoken with Zar-Thule, a barbarian reaver—or rather, with the fumbling mushroom *thing* that had once been a reaver—locked away in Klühn's deepest dungeon to rot and gibber hideously of unearthly horrors. For Zar-Thule had thought to rob the House of Cthulhu on Arlyeh the forbidden isle, as a result of which Arlyeh had gone down under the waves in a great storm...but not before Zar-Thule gazed upon Cthulhu, whose treasures were garnets of green slime, red rubies of blood and moonstones of malignancy and madness!

And when dreams such as those conjured by Zar-Thule's story came to sour the sweet embrace of Shoosh, Goddess of the Still Slumbers, I would rise from my couch and tremble, and pace the crystal floors of my rooms above the Bay of Klühn. For I was sorely troubled by this mystery; even I, Teh Atht, whose peer in the occult arts exists not in Theem'hdra, troubled most sorely...

So I went up into the Mount of the Ancients where I smoked the Zha-weed and sought the advice of my wizard ancestor Mylakhrion of Tharamoon—dead eleven hundred years—who told me to look to the ORIGIN and the AFTERMATH, the BEGINNING and the END, that I might know. And that same night, in my secret vault, I sipped a rare and bitter distillation of mandrake and descended again into deepest dreams, even into dreams long dead and forgotten before ever human dreamers existed. Thus in my search for the ORIGIN I dreamed myself into the dim and fabulous past.

And I saw that the Earth was hot and in places molten, and Gleeth was not yet born to sail the volcanic clouds of pre-dawn nights. Then, drawn by a force beyond my ken, I went out into the empty spaces of the primal void, where I saw, winging down through the vasty dark, shapes of uttermost lunacy. And first among them all was Cthulhu of the tentacled face, and among His followers came Yogg-Sothoth, Tsathoggua, and many others which were like unto Cthulhu but less than Him; and lo!—Cthulhu spoke the Name of Azathoth, whereupon stars blazed forth as He passed and all space gloried in His coming.

Down through the outer immensities they winged, alighting upon the steaming Earth and building great cities of a rare architecture, wherein singular angles confused the eye and mind until towers were as precipices and solid walls gateways! And there they dwelt for aeons, in their awful cities under leaden skies and strange stars. Aye, and they were mighty sorcerers, Cthulhu and His spawn, who plotted great evil against Others who were once their brethren. For they had not come to Earth of their own will but had fled from Elder Gods whose codes they had abused most terribly.

And such were their thaumaturgies in the great grey cities that those Elder Gods felt tremors in the very stuff of Existence itself, and they came in haste and great anger to set seals on the houses of Cthulhu, wherein He and many of His kin were prisoned for their sins. But others of these great old sorcerers, such as Yogg-Sothoth and Yibb-Tstll, fled again into the stars, where they were followed by the Elder Gods who prisoned them wherever they were found. Then, when all was done, the great and just Gods of Eld returned whence they had come; and aeon upon aeon passed and the stars revolved through strange configurations, moving inexorably toward a time when Cthulhu would be set free…

So it was that I saw the ORIGIN whereof my ancestor Mylakhrion of Tharamoon had advised me, and awakening in my secret vault I shuddered and marvelled that this Loathly Lord Cthulhu had come down all the ages unaltered. For I knew that indeed He lived still in His city sunken under the sea, and I was mazed by His immortality. Then it came to me to dwell at length upon the latter; on Cthulhu's immortality, and to wonder if He was truly immortal…. And of this also had Mylakhrion counselled me, saying, "Look to the ORIGIN and the AFTERMATH, the BEGINNING and the END."

Thus it was that last night I sipped again of mandrake fluid and went out in a dream to seek the END. And indeed I found it…

There at the end of time all was night, where all the universe was a great empty tomb and nothing stirred. And I stood upon a dead sea bottom and looked up to where Gleeth had once graced the skies; old Gleeth, long sundered now and drifted down to Earth as dust. And I turned my saddened eyes down again to gaze upon a gaunt, solitary spire of rock that rose and twisted and towered up from the bottom of the dusty ocean.

And because curiosity was ever the curse of sorcerers, it came to me to wonder why, since this was the END, time itself continued to exist. And it further came to me that time existed only because space, time's brother, had *not quite* ended, life was *not quite* extinct. With this thought, as if born of the thought itself, there came a mighty rumbling and the ground trembled and shook. All the world shuddered and the dead sea bottom split open in many places, creating chasms from which there at once rose up the awful spawn of Cthulhu!

And lo!—I knew now that indeed Cthulhu was immortal, for in Earth's final death spasm He was reborn! The great twisted spire of rock—all that was left of Arlyeh, Cthulhu's house—shattered and fell in ruins, laying open to my staggering gaze His sepulchre. And shortly thereafter, preceded by a nameless stench, He squeezed Himself out from the awful tomb into the gloom of the dead universe.

Then, when they saw Cthulhu, all of them that were risen up from their immemorial prisons rushed and flopped and floundered to His feet, making obeisance to Him. And He blinked great evil octopus eyes and gazed all about in wonderment, for His final sleep had endured for aeon upon aeon, and he had not known that the universe was now totally dead and time itself at an end.

And Cthulhu's anger was great! He cast His mind out into the void and gazed upon cinders that had been stars; He looked for light and warmth in the farthest corners of the universe and found only darkness and decay; He searched for life in the great seas of space and found only the tombs at time's end. And His anger waxed *awesome!*

Then He threw back His tentacled head and bellowed out the Name of Azathoth in a voice that sent all of the lesser Beings at His feet scurrying back to their chasm sepulchres, and lo!… nothing happened! The sands of time were run out, and even the greatest Magicks had lost their potency.

And so Cthulhu raged and stormed and blasphemed as only He might until, at the height of His anger, *suddenly He knew me!*

Dreaming as I was and far, far removed from my own age, nevertheless He sensed me and in an instant turned upon me, face tentacles writhing and reaching out for my dreaming spirit. And then, to my eternal damnation, before I fled shrieking back down the corridors of time to leap awake drenched in a chill perspiration in my secret vault, I gazed deep into the demon eyes of Cthulhu.

Now it is dawn and I am almost done with the writing of this, and soon I will lay down my rune-book and set myself certain tasks for the days ahead. First I will see to it that the crystal dome of my workshop tower is covered with black lacquer, for I fear I can no longer bear to look out upon the stars…. Where once they twinkled afar in chill but friendly fashion, now I know that they leer down in celestial horror as they move inexorably toward Cthulhu's next awakening. For surely He will rise up many times before that final awakening at the very END.

Aye, and if I had thought to escape the Lord of Arlyeh when I fled from him in my dream, then I was mistaken. Cthulhu was, He is, and He will always be; and I know now that this is the essence of that great mystery which so long perplexed me. For Cthulhu is a Master of Dreams, and now He knows me. And He will follow me through my slumbers all the days of my life, and evermore I shall hear His call—

—Even unto THE END.

MOTHER LOVE

Wouldn't you know it? Another problem child. Hah!

With a high-pitched whine the bullet took a long groove out of the rock wall to his right, showering him with sharp splinters. He flung himself awkwardly to the ground, feeling a splash of blood on his face where one of the hot, flying fragments had caught him. Simultaneous with the second crack of the rifle, another bullet kicked up dirt in his eyes with a buzz and a thud as it buried itself in the ground a few inches in front of his nose. He waited for a few seconds, blood pounding, before peering cautiously from his prone position along the narrow rock passage to where the girl stood—tattered denims moulding the fine shape of her wide-spread legs—squinting down the sights of her weapon...sights which were centered squarely on him!

"Lady, if you're planning to scare me, you've done it already. If you're trying to kill me, aim a little more carefully—I just hate the thought of bleeding to death." His voice carried to her, a hoarse, panting shout as she began to squeeze the trigger for the third shot. She eased her finger slowly out of the trigger-guard to leave it lying there, a thought's distance from sudden death.

"What are you after?" The way she said it—menacing, low so he could hardly hear—it was more than a question; it was a warning, and he knew he would have to answer carefully. Only sixty feet separated them and there was nowhere he could run. If she was any good at all with that rifle she could put a neat hole right through his head before he made five or six feet.

"Lady, I seen your fire-smoke earlier in the day, and I smelled your cooking a mile off. Smelled pretty good to a man who hasn't ate in three, days—and when I did last eat it was a rat I was lucky enough to catch!" His panting came a little easier now. "But lady, if you want me to move on…you just say the word and I'll be on my way. I'd be plenty obliged, though, if you'd allow me a bite to eat first."

"Get up," she ordered. As he climbed to his feet she stared at the stump where his right arm should have been. "You can't be a mutant—you're too old for that."

He walked slowly, carefully up the defile, dusting himself off as he went towards the girl who was outlined, now, against the evening greens and browns of the small valley behind her. She had a nice set-up here, and she was alone—otherwise she wouldn't be toting that rifle herself. As he drew closer to her he saw the cave on the other side of the valley. Could hardly be more than a hundred yards across, that valley; more a saddle between the hills. Corn patch growing nicely… mutant strawberries…rabbits. She had real good legs…

She saw where he was looking.

"Hold it right there." He came to a halt not ten feet away from her. "I asked you a question!" She swung the rifle to point it significantly at his middle.

"Mutant? No, industrial accident, that's all—long before the war," he answered. "But I've been given the mutant treatment ever since. So has every cripple! Been kicked out of every town I ever went near for almost four years. It's no fun, lady—'specially now they're burnin' mutants! Look, if you've any decency at all, you'll give me just a bite of what you've got cooking over there, and then I'll be on my way."

She thought about it, began to shake her head negatively, then changed her mind: "You're… welcome—but I'll warn you now, there's three unmarked graves in the corners of this valley. You try anything…I'll have no more corners left." She waved him past with the gun, taking a good look at him as he went. He was about thirty-five, forty perhaps. He'd probably put on age fast after the war. Feeling her eyes on his stump, he glanced back over his shoulder.

"Armless, I be," he said in wry humour, gratified to see her relax a little. Then: "How come you're up here on your own?

You've been here some years by the look of the place."

"I lived in the town on the coast back there, where the walls shine at night," she gestured vaguely behind her. "That place at the foot of the hills, just a heap of rubble now, you must have come through it to get up here. I was only eighteen then... when the war came. One of the first bombs landed in the sea, threw radioactive water all over the town. When my baby was born he was—different. The radiation..." She faltered, lost for words. "...My husband died quickly. What few people lived through it wanted to have my baby put...they wanted to kill him. Said it would be better for him. Said it would be better for both of us. I ran off. I stole the rifle, shells, some seeds and one or two other odds and ends. Been here ever since. I get along fine..."

"You still got the mut...?" But he knew that was a mistake before the word was out. The air seemed to go hard.

"Mister," she poked the barrel of the gun viciously between his shoulder blades, "if you're a mutant-hunter you're as good as dead!" He staggered from the pressure of the rifle in his back, turning to face her, going suddenly white as he saw her finger tightening on the trigger.

"No ...! No, just curious. Christ, I've been hunted myself—and it's obvious I couldn't be a mutant! What, me? A mutant-hunter! Why, some places there's a bounty, sure, but out here in the middle of nowhere? I mean...do I look like a bounty hunter...?" He was pathetic.

She relaxed again. "My baby...he...he died! No more questions." It was an order.

They had crossed the valley and the sun was starting to sink behind the hills. He peered eagerly into the pot hanging over the fire. The cave was a dark blot behind the glowing embers, with a homemade candle flickering at its back.

This was sure a good thing she'd got, he mused to himself, licking his lips.

She motioned with the rifle, indicating he should help himself from the pot. He took up a battered tin plate and heaped it with the thick, bubbling stew before dropping the heavy iron spoon back into the pot. Juicy rabbit bones protruded from the meat in the mess of stew on his plate. Without another word he started eating. It was good.

As he ate he looked the girl over. She had a good face to match her figure. He could hardly keep from staring at the way her shirt swelled outwards with the pressure of the firm breasts beneath it. And it was that above all else—the way her shirt strained from her body—which finally decided his course of action.

He licked his lips and reached casually for the spoon again, crouching with the plate on his knees...

In a second he had straightened and the hot stuff was on her neck. Before she even had time to yelp from the shock he had brought her a savage, whiplash, back-hand blow across the face with the swing of a powerfully muscled left arm. As she spun sideways he nimbly grabbed the falling rifle out of midair and turned it on her. She started to scramble to her feet, a red welt already blossoming on her face.

"Stay put!" He held the rifle loosely in his hand, confident finger on the trigger, daring her to make a false move. "I'll shoot you in the legs," he said, grinning wolfishly, "so's not to spoil you completely. You wouldn't want to be spoiled completely, now would you?"

She cringed away from him on the ground. "You wouldn't... you—"

"Get up!" he snarled, the grin sliding from his face.

As she made to get to her feet he tossed the rifle behind him and slammed another roundly swinging blow to her face. She lurched backwards, falling, and before she could recover he stepped over her, planting his feet firmly, tearing the shirt from her supple body. "Thing was ready to bust anyway..."

He licked his lips again as she screamed and tried to cover herself. "Shirt sure didn't tell no lie..."

He grabbed her left wrist, twisting her arm up behind her back, forcing her to her feet.

"Sweetheart, your feeding's good—now let's see what your loving's like. The good Lord knows you've probably waited a long time!"

"Don't...! Don't do it. I fed you, I..."

"More fool you, sweetheart," he rasped, cutting her off, "but you may's well get used to me; I'm going to be here quite some time. You need a man about the place."

He pushed her into the cave, noting that the candle at the rear stood beside a heavy black blanket, stretched luxuriously in a hollow on the floor.

The shadows moved in the dimness of the cave as he shoved her towards the sputtering candle. A few feet from the rear wall of rock she twisted under her own arm and pulled away from him. He laughed at the way her body moved as she tried to free herself. "No good getting all hot and bothered now, sweetheart—not with the bed all laid out for us..."

"It's not a bed!" she screamed, jerking her arm back in desperate resistance. The sweat of anticipation on his straining fingers let him down. Her hand suddenly slipped through his and he crashed backwards, off balance, onto the 'bed.'

There was instant, horrible movement beneath him.

"No...!" the girl screamed. "No! That's not stew, Baby, it's a man!"

But Baby, who had no ears, took no notice.

The edges of the 'bed' rose up in thickly glistening, black doughy flaps—like an inky, folding pancake—and flopped purposefully over the struggling man upon it. Subtly altered digestive juices squirted into his face and muscular hardness gripped him. He gave a shriek—just one—as the living envelope around him started to squeeze.

Hours later, when dawn was spreading like a pale stain over the horizon between the hills, the girl was still crying. Baby had taken a long time over his meal. He burped, ejecting the last bone and a few odd buttons. There wasn't even a back she could pat him on.

That day there was a new grave in the little valley in the hills. A very small one...

NOT A CREATURE WAS STIRRING

But what if it does?

Not even a mouse—maybe nothing at all—but I had got out of bed anyway just to be sure. And now instead of the sound of Silver Bells jingling away in my head, there were these great gonging brass ones, and some blinding fireworks, too!

I managed to get my right arm untwisted from behind my back where I'd fallen on it, and slowly, carefully put up my hand to touch my scalp three to four inches above my right ear. Just a touch but it stung like the blazes and left my fingers sticky with the blood that was still oozing from the gash. As for my left arm: maybe it was broken—likewise from the fall, I supposed—because even moving it a fraction was painful. What's more, when I tried to lift my head up from the floor the carpet tugged at a patch of my hair that was stuck down. I always heal quickly and the blood was already drying, which meant I'd only been out for maybe twenty minutes maximum. So at least I wasn't going to bleed to death.

As the cracked bells and searing fireworks in my head eased up a little, I began to think more clearly. And I wondered about Maria, my lady friend. You might say she was my fiancée, even though we'd made no real plans so far. Maria had been sleeping like a baby when I got up to investigate what I thought was the furtive sound of someone at the front door of the house; definitely *not* someone coming down the chimney! Whatever, I had told myself, most likely it was only my overly sensitive ears; and it *was* very wintry outside. Every so often I could hear the rattle of a length of dangling, broken trellising clattering against the frame of the kitchen window, the way it always did when it was windy. However, I had considered it better to be safe than sorry.

But about Maria:

Yes, she was all warm, cuddly and fast asleep in bed, where I should be. But last night—the *actual* night before Christmas, because it was well into the wee small hours now, which made it Christmas Day morning—had been a very special night. I mean, I don't usually brag about such, but when we were done she'd been worn to a frazzle and, truth to tell, me too. All of which had been on my mind as I got downstairs, yawning and stumbling and already cursing myself for a fool, *because* Maria was still in bed and I wasn't…then cursing myself for an even bigger fool (when I suddenly sensed the shadows stirring as something stepped out of the darkness) I paid for my weariness and customary carelessness in instantaneous pain.

And going down like a felled tree, I had thought: "I should have brought a torch with me, or put on the landing light or something…" But my eyes were usually keen at night—I might say exceptionally so—except when they were full of sleep or booze, or pretty much glazed over from too much sex.

Anyway, there I lay nursing my sore head while the last few Catherine-wheels slowly sputtered to a standstill, still trying to figure out how badly hurt I was without attracting too much attention from our uninvited guest or guests, gradually cranking my head up from the carpet without yanking on too many bloody hairs and starting the bleeding going again. At which point a nervously active electric torch beam quit swinging here and there and went out, and one of the ceiling lights came on.

The fellow with the cosh—a piece of piping tucked in his belt, no doubt with my blood still drying on it—was standing there against the wall with one hand on a light switch while the index finger on his other hand wagged a no-no at me and moved quickly to his lips in a signal that was unmistakable. He had seen that my eyes were open—had probably seen how I was moving, barely—and was telling me to stay still and keep quiet. And while in my dazed and damaged condition there seemed little or no need for him to emphasize this unspoken warning, still he did so by scowling in a sinister fashion, and with his hand falling to his cosh took a single menacing step closer.

Also—and in case I still hadn't understood the threat he presented, or so I imagined—in a harsh whisper he said: "No noise, no trouble, and there'll be no more hurting. But if you give me trouble, I mean *any* trouble at all, I'll simply bash your fucking brains in! Got it?" In answer to which:

"Got it," I whispered or croaked back at him. And I didn't even try nodding.

The light he had put on was one of several whose sockets were sunk in the ceiling. They provided ample illumination when lit in series but were only dim individually. Just this one, however, would be more than enough to allow him to continue with his work...which, quite obviously was to rob me. Well, good luck to him, because there wasn't a hell of a lot here for him to rob...which probably meant bad luck for me, because he might well want to take his disappointment out on someone or thing or me in a violent fashion. And, since you can't ever tell about someone like this thug just how far his eventual reaction will go once it dawns on him there's little or no profit in his night's work, now I was glad that Maria was still asleep and not attracting any unwanted attention...

As he took another step toward me I finally managed to lift my head an inch or two from the floor without passing out again, and from that angle I now had a somewhat better view of my assailant. I immediately recognized him and remembered where I'd seen him before: that had been late yesterday afternoon, Christmas Eve, at the kennels. We had been down there, Maria and I, handing out one or two small gifts and paying Christmas bonuses to the team of men I have working for me. No Christmas break for them: when you take care of dogs that people have left in your safe-keeping while they go off on holiday or whatever, you're on duty all day long—nights too, if an animal gets sick. But what with walkies and exercising, cleaning bowls and prepping food, regulating the feeding and watering times, mucking out the cages, making sure the kennels are clean and warm, and organizing medications for any of the mutts with worms or other problems—it's a full-time job! Not for me, because these are my kennels and I'm the boss, but definitely for my dog-handlers.

And that was where I'd seen this guy before, in the company of a second rough- and somehow suspicious-looking character: at the kennels talking to my foreman. I had taken the pair for potential customers, but since the kennels are always full this time of year I'd known they would get turned away and hadn't interfered. By then the evening had been drawing in and it was starting to get dark early, the way it does this time of year; so we'd driven home to my converted barn of a place on the edge of dense woodlands, and I'd given it no more thought. But now I also remembered how during that short drive home another car had stayed maybe a hundred yards behind us, driving on dipped lights. As I'd turned into the driveway, however, this other car had sped on by, vanishing up the road. Which was fine and I hadn't been too concerned; it's just that it's a lonely road, that's all. And out in the sticks like that our home is a lonely sort of place...

But as for now:

Well, obviously I should have been concerned. And now too I wondered: where had this vicious thug's equally unpleasant-looking partner got to? As if in answer to which the main door opened to let in a single blast of cold night air, along with the very fellow in question, quickly closing the door behind him and none too quietly.

"Aren't you supposed to be watching the road?" thug number one whispered harshly, as thug number two paced into my living-room and gazed down on me.

"It's cold out there, Joe," number two replied, not bothering to whisper. "It could freeze the balls off a brass monkey! Also, I don't know what I'm doing out there. I mean, there's nothing on that road in daylight hours, let alone this time of night on a Christmas morning! You think maybe Santa is going to come by? So I decided to come in and find out what's keeping you. It's been almost half an hour, Joe!"

"Oh, that's great, just great! Thanks a bunch!" said Joe, sarcastically. "So now he's heard my name twice...*Freddie!*"

"Oh, yeah! My mistake—sorry," said Freddie, taken aback.

And then: "But was there any need for that? I mean, you giving him my name, too? Because what with our form, our names and descriptions…"

"We'll get picked up before you can say Fanny's your aunt!" Joe snarled. And because he was angry now, he wasn't being any too quiet either.

"Which means—" said Freddie, only to be cut off short by the other's—

"Yeah, we know what that means: we can't leave any witnesses, so the house will have to be torched. A Christmas bonfire, right? Well, there's a nice tree in the kitchen. It looks out on the garden and the road, or it would if the drapes were open. But these people—" he scowled at me, "—it's as if they're into seclusion or something…and how! Living out here at the arse end of nowhere, and every window heavily draped; not even a chink of light coming in from outside…" And then, more thoughtfully: "As for that tree, it's all tinsel, decorations and what have you. So maybe the fire should be electrical, right? An electrical fault—you know?"

"Yeah, sure, I can fix that," said Freddie, nodding eagerly. "And no one will ever know the difference. But…a tree? With expensive presents, maybe?"

"Not a one," Joe rasped. "I've been right through the house, downstairs at least, and apart from that tree—which can only be for show, letting people like us know there's somebody home, even when there isn't—this place might as well be a fucking cave! Oh, there's the usual kitchen shit, a wardrobe full of fairly expensive clothing, most of it the woman's, and a bureau full of paperwork and bills from his kennels. But as for anything else…"

And now Freddie suddenly came alive, his eyes gleaming (with an almost feral light, I thought) as I chanced moving, stretching and easing cramped muscles, and doing my best to make myself a little more comfortable…at least until Freddie grinned and licked his lips, and said: "Oh, yeah, the woman! I'd almost forgotten about her. But if you haven't been upstairs yet, maybe I should go up and check it out. She could be awake; she could know we're here, and she's just waiting and hoping we'll go away. But what if there's a telephone up there? Yeah, I should go on up. And in the event there's nothing worth taking...I mean, I'd really hate to waste a good looking bitch like her. Oh, sure, let's *waste* her by all means, but *taste* her first, right?" And:

Skinny bastard! I thought. If anyone was going to call Maria a bitch it was me, and even I would have to be careful! That sort of bad-mouthing didn't go down too well with any female I ever knew, no matter her colour, creed or persuasions. And meanwhile Joe was saying:

"Okay, go on up. But try to remember the rules: profits first—if there's any to be had—and the, er, bonuses come last. And Freddie, when you're done you might also remember to give me a call, right?" With which he sniggered, but Freddie was already halfway upstairs...

Well, I wasn't about to let anything like *that* happen, so growling my pain and anger I sat up and tried to rise. No use, I was simply hurting too much. And with his cosh in his hand, Joe was on me in a flash; or would have been, but this time I was ready for him. Tripping him with my right leg, I managed to kick him in the groin with my left; it was as much as I could do. He didn't fall, but as he bent almost double and went staggering and cursing across the room, so, from upstairs came a series of astonished, first questioning, then angry yelps from Maria. Having forgotten the rules, Freddie had woken her up and was trying for the bonus.

But at last fortune was turning in our favour. For finally going to his knees, Joe had tried to steady himself by grabbing at the drapes in the bay windows. That proved too much for the wooden curtain rings, which broke apart under the sudden extra weight. And down came those heavy drapes on top of Joe, and in came the moonlight—the silvery *full* moonlight!

By which time the screams from upstairs—Freddie's screams, that is—had become pretty much deafening, only to fade and quickly die away as Maria's growling and slavering grew louder. She must have somehow fought her way to a window and let the moonlight into our bedroom. And with the drapes opened up it had been "curtains" for Freddie—if you'll pardon the pun. For while sunlight is fatal to vampires, full moonlight, which sometimes happens at this time of year, has the opposite effect on us guys. And in no time at all I was back in shape—my *other* shape, you understand—where except for a couple of bruises I was all healed up.

So what else can I tell you? I had an early Christmas morning breakfast, and when Maria came loping downstairs I was just finishing off.

"Well, *that* was a nice surprise," she said, her tongue lolling and her jaws all red. "Just as I was getting hungry, and thinking maybe it was a mistake to fast over Christmas, this happens. So now tell me, you didn't perhaps send Santa a letter up the chimney, right?"

"Heck, no!" said I, holding back a howl of laughter. "It's just the way things worked out, that's all. I mean, surely you know how all that weird Christmas mythology leaves me cold?

And anyway, where in hell could I have got us a pair of stockings that big, eh?"

IN THE GLOW ZONE

Best to stay out of there, is all!

Mommy is dead.

She is dead and there is no water and no rats left. The water has turned very hard and thick now so we can't fish. And we can't dig roots because the ground is hard too. There was cold-white when we woke up and found Mommy dead. That was three days. She is cold and thin and stiff and still. She is dead. She is like the rats we trap or throw stones at when they are dead. Except they are sometimes fat and she is very thin...

We all cried when we saw her. She had told us she would be dead soon. When the rats were all gone from round here before the water went hard and the cold-white she said it. She told us I am going into town for rats I will be back soon. If I don't come back keep warm. Eat roots and rats and drink river water. Try to find clothes in the villages—*and keep away from men!*

Before she went to town she said this will be the death of me. She meant the Green Glow. Nobody lives in the town, it is all broken down and at night there is the Green Glow. We can see it now fading as the sky gets bright. Mommy is sitting in the corner all stiff and cold. She has a Green Glow too now.

Before she died she said you are to eat me if you get too hungry but please bury my bones and make a little cross to mark the place. We think she did not know what she said. We will not eat her, we would not like that and anyway she has the Green Glow. We never ate rats with the Green Glow and we will not eat Mommy. She once told us the Green Glow is your father, it is more your father than the rotten bastard who ran off on me when the war started. *Men are all bastards* she told us.

When she came back from town we ate. She had small rats and one very big one she called a cat. There were more cats she said but all mutants. This one was a very old cat from before the war. He remembered people and went to her so she could hit him with her axe…the axe is ours now she is dead.

She roasted some rats and we ate but soon she was sick. Next day her hair came out. Next day it came out a lot and blood too. Then she said the Green Glow has got me and I will die.

And she did. And three days are gone and the rats too and the cold-white is here and we are hungry.

Over there is smoke. It has nearly always been there. Mommy only made fires at night. She said she knew the Woman and Her Two who made the fire. She said she had met them long ago when we were little. The Woman was nice but Mommy was frightened of Her Two. They were not sensible they were like animals Mommy said. They aren't like you she said they bit like rats.

The smoke is still there but it is quiet now. Before there was sometimes noise. When there was noise Mommy said they were hunting for food the Woman and Her Two. Then she would make us hide but nobody ever came here…

The Woman and Her Two are very quiet now. Perhaps they are dead like Mommy. We think the *men* got them *men* and their dogs. Dogs are like rats but even bigger than cats Mommy told us. We couldn't see the dogs much but we heard them making loud angry noises. We saw the *men* a lot of them running through the village over there. They had ropes and we saw things jumping on the ropes where the cold-white was deep following the men. Because the cold-white is deep we couldn't see the dogs very well but they jumped and made angry noises and we heard them.

We heard the Woman too she was crying very loud and Her Two were making noises like the dogs. That was before dark. In the night the *men* laughed and the Woman made very bad noises. Now there is no noise but the smoke is more than before. We think the *men* made a big fire before they left. The cold-white is falling but over there we still see the smoke.

We know all *men* are bastards because Mommy said so and she said what the bastards would do to us if they found us. We think they did it to the Woman and Her Two. We will only light our fire at night. Then the *men* and their dogs will stay out of the Glow Zone...

Once before when it was warm and there were roots and some fat rats and a few fish a *man* found us. He was a bastard.

When Mommy saw him coming she said hide and we did. He didn't see us right off but we could see him. He didn't say a lot but we knew Mommy was frightened she was frightened of the *man*. We never saw a *man* before he was a lot like Mommy. He had a stick-thing. Mommy gave him some fish to eat and showed him a place to sleep when he was asleep she came to us and said he might be OK you stay there and when he wakes up he might go away. Don't let him see you she said. She said he has a gun it is that stick-thing he carries it can kill very quick.

While she was talking the *man* got up and came over. He said what you got there and shoved Mommy out of the way. Then he said Goddamn might have known it a girl like you alone in the Glow Zone well you treat me right and there'll be no trouble.

He caught hold of Mommy's hair and started to pull her and we moved at him. He looked very frightened he pointed the stick-thing Mommy said no stay where you are it's all right. We knew it wasn't...

It got dark soon we stayed where we were and listened to the funny noises in the dark. The *man* was making a lot of little noises and Mommy was crying but quietly. It was very dark when she came to us she said go get the axe the bastard's really asleep this time we'll kill him but let me get his gun first.

We got the axe she got his gun and he came awake. Mommy stood back and we got hold of him quick before he could stand and hit him in the body with the axe. No no Mommy said his head get his head. He was shouting oh my god my god we hit him in the head. There was a lot of blood.

Next morning Mommy said we won't bury such as him he'll feed the fish so we took him to the river. His body moved slow in the water towards town right in the middle of the Glow Zone.

Serve the bastard right Mommy said.

It is very cold we think of a fire. A fire will bring *men* but not if we use the Woman and Her Two's fire. We think they must be dead. Anyway we are cold.

We go to where the smoke rises through the cold-white. Nearly there we find things we think they must be the Woman's Two. They are dead and stiff there is a lot of blood and little holes in them. We see how they look and remember what Mommy said we are glad they are dead. The Woman is near the fire she has no clothes she is stiff and cold. There is blood on her face and body she looks a lot like Mommy and we are sad. She is dead. There is a cave in a big heap of bricks it has a blanket hanging at the front. The Woman and Her Two lived there we think. We move towards the cave perhaps it is warm.

There is a loud dog noise a dog jumps at us through the cold-white. We grab him and hit with the axe he is dead. A *man* comes through the blanket in front of the cave he says *what the hell.*

Jesus Christ boys lookee here. He points his stick-thing called a gun and we rush at him. We are angry all *men* are bastards. There is a very loud noise and we are hurt. We are hit in our body and the gun has smoke but we don't stop running on all our hands and legs. The *man* points his gun again but we are on him. We knock down the gun we swing our axe at his head. There is blood on the cold-white the *man* is down we stamp on him.

The blanket is torn down other *men* the *men* from last night are there they have guns. All the guns are making loud noises and we are hurt very bad in the body. One *man* turns to run when we are near and we hit him hard our axe sticks in his back when he falls he makes loud noises.

One other bastard says great god in…will you look at what a bloody—look out! We rush at him but the guns are loud and there is much blood from our body and too much hurt. We jump on the *man* and pull an arm off him and stomp on him.

Now there are dogs jumping and they have teeth. We are torn the guns hurt we fall down in the cold-white it is red now.

One of our heads is hit we hurt so much we crash all our arms and legs.

Our body is all red we are very tired.

Another head is hit.

Another...We will soon be dead our body will be stiff and cold.

Like Mommy...

LITTLE MAN LOST

Location! Location! But how to make sure it's the right one?

Lost! Howard Pratt paused, looked up and down the street, frowned and shook his head. Most Definitely lost. Ridiculous!

Lost—*again!*

He remembered when he was a small boy: how in a big store one day he had wandered off amidst the endless shelves of toys, and how in a very little while he'd became lost. Lost in lingerie, in electrical appliances, in linens and silks and satins. Gone!

Gone from the world of his mother, for of course his mother had *been* the world to a very small, very frightened Howard. And he remembered the screams (his screams) and the hot tears, the frantic running and stumbling and panting and stamping, the temper-cum-panic tantrum that hadn't seemed to work…before at last she found him; came and took him from the strange arms of a strange store lady, back into *her* familiar warmth and smell; and used the hankie that also smelled just right, for him to blow his nose on. And how he had never, *ever* strayed from her side for, oh, for a long time after that.

Twenty years later, of course, he had lost her permanently, and then there had been more tears. But no screams, no foot-stamping. Oh, something inside had stamped and screamed— as her oblong box slid smoothly into the all-consuming flames, to the tune of some unheard-of hymn—but by then Howard had been a man and hysterics weren't his scene. And anyway, in the interim he'd found himself a wife, grown used to *her* smell, *her* warmth. So with his mother's death, well, that wasn't quite the same. He hadn't been lost that time. He'd lost something, yes, but not himself.

His world was still there. He had a home, however small, however Spartan (for Howard wasn't a rich man), and a wife, a job, a hobby, places to be and other places to go. And he had known who he was. That was the essence of it: one could never really be lost as long as one retained one's identity.

And he had never thought about being lost, and he had certainly never feared it, and he had rarely if ever remembered that time from long ago when as a small he'd actually been lost—until now.

Lost…

It was so silly he could almost chuckle, except he hadn't done that since Mildred left. Since when he had seemed to get himself lost far too often. And when one considered that one had lived here all one's life…

Children—he nodded, biting his lip, still peering up and down the street and wondering which way he should go—*there should have been children.* For now he had no one. And if there had been children, perhaps Mildred wouldn't have left. Actually, he still didn't know why she had done it—or who with.

Oh, yes, that was a possibility.

Maybe she'd met someone else. No children, no ties, nothing behind her and (far worse), nothing much to look forward to. She had felt…lost.

Suddenly, remembering, Howard gave a start. Yes, she had said that—several times, in fact—but he hadn't really been listening. They didn't listen to each other very much, not toward the end. Not for years. But he remembered now: how often she had said she felt…lost. And how often she'd looked it.

Howard turned up his collar against a chill wind that blew plastic bags and autumn leaves and flapping pages of discarded newspapers down the street, buttoned his coat fumblingly and walked on a little more hurriedly. At the next junction he turned right, telling himself that he did so out of instinct.

Of course, he knew *why* he got lost so easily these days. It was simply that his mind wasn't on what he did. He allowed himself to wander too much. Upstairs, he wandered. He didn't have his shit together (that's how it might be expressed in modern jargon). Absent-minded. But only because his mind had so much to dwell upon, was full of so many things to distract him. So he told himself.

Except it was getting worse.

Howard missed busses, missed underground trains; and when he did manage to catch them, missed his stops. That was what had happened today: missed his stop, gone too far on the underground, got off at the next station instead. Of course, he could have simply caught the next train back, but experience had shown him that didn't always work...

Fresh air, a brisk walk—why, he hadn't been up this way in years! And he wasn't *really* lost, now was he? What, within half-a-mile of his own home? Where he'd lived for the last eighteen years...with Mildred?

She *had* looked lost, and said she felt it. Maybe he should have paid more attention. Perhaps he should pay more attention to other things, before they too...left him.

For a moment panic struck at Howard. He wanted to run, barely managed to control himself. But run where?

Or was it possible he'd lost himself deliberately? Maybe he'd subconsciously hoped that, in going into streets he didn't know, sooner or later he'd find Mildred. Obviously she wouldn't go where she knew he went, but she might well be where he shouldn't be! On the other hand, she could be on the other side of the moon for all he knew. For all he cared...?

No, that was unfair. On Howard. He had *liked* Mildred. Why, eighteen years ago he'd thought he loved her! Maybe liking wasn't enough. Maybe she'd wanted more than that, wanted to *be* someone. She had used to go on about her identity a lot, toward the end. About who she was—or wasn't.

That was the entire trick of it, surely: knowing one's *direction*, knowing who one was, not getting lost.

The street was like a canyon now, its houses rising up on both sides like cliffs; unscalable, unknown and unknowable. And it was getting dark. Howard wandered in a darkening land; down dirty, wind-blown canyons of dust and leaves, newspaper pages and dog-dirt; and most intimidating of all the bleary windows and doors and walls of houses—all alike, house upon house, unending—like the rows of stacked shelves in some superstore. Houses like boxes, or packages…like suits, shirts and costumes, ties and toys, toiletries and cosmetics and cutlery and—

LOST!

Ma-ma! He felt it welling inside. *Ma-maaaa!*

Something bumped into him, caught at him, steadied him.

"'Ere, mate! You OK?" A big man, frowning. Not angry, concerned. At least, Howard hoped so.

"All right?" he repeated the man's query. "Oh, yes—fine! But—"

"Yers?"

But Howard could only answer the stranger in the merest whisper, choked before it could fashion a single word. Drowned in tears and wetly stillborn.

"Eh, wot? 'Ere, you *cryin'*?"

Howard tried it again, clung to the stranger, fought to hold down the lump rising in his throat, hold back the wail in his voice, unclench the acid knot in his stomach. And finally said: "Lost!"

"Lost?" The big man stared at him, tightened his grip on Howard's shoulders. "Huh? *That's* nothing new! Done it meself. Do it all the time, I do. The older we gets, the dafter, I always say. Lost, yers. Well, where do you want to be?" He peered closer from beneath bushy eyebrows.

"Garling Street," Howard whispered. "Just off The Broadway."

"Garling? Ho, well!" said the other. "First right, down there—" he pointed, "—then second left and right again—and you're there!"

"Really?" Howard got something of a grip on himself.

"Garling, yers—know it well," said the big man. "Used to, anyway."

"Well, thank you," said Howard, turning away.

"Ere!" The big man grabbed him again. "Not so fast, mate." It was quite dark now, and no one on the street. The odd light gleamed through hedges from behind grimy windows, like the eyes of great cats waiting to pounce. "Maybe, seeing as 'ow I 'elped you, you can 'elp me?"

"I have no money," Howard cringed.

"Money?" the big man stared. For the first time Howard noticed how the stranger's Adam's apple wobbled, the catch in his gruff voice, the way his hands shook where they gripped his shoulders. "Not money, mate, no! Wot? Yer fink I'm a mugger? Me? No, not me. But…"

"Yes?" Howard prompted him.

"Queen Street," said the man—a little gaspingly, Howard thought. And he remembered a sign he'd seen on the corner house where he'd made his last turn.

"But…this *is* Queen Street!" he said.

"Eh? Wot?" Disbelief, then relief, flooded the other's square face. He released Howard, turned, looked all about in the darkness, seemed to stagger. "Why, bless me!"

Howard backed away.

"Bless me!" the man said again. He reeled against a garden gate, straightened up, gave a choked little laugh. The gate opened at his touch. Without looking back, he walked swayingly down the garden path, let himself into the house. Lights went on. He obviously lived there!

Howard gaped, then turned and ran.

Narrow escape. A loony. At this time of night. And no one on the streets. A narrow escape!

Howard turned right, second left, right again—and was there! Just like the man had said. Garling Street. Where he'd lived for eighteen years. With Mildred…

Number 27. Howard let himself in, put on the light, sat down. His heart was hammering. Tomorrow he'd see a doctor. He was ill. He *had* to be ill. Eighteen years, and he could get lost a hundred yards from home! And so often! Howard couldn't hold it back any longer; he began to sob in earnest.

Where—*when* had it started? How? Why?

With Mildred's leaving? No, before that. Why, he'd even got lost going to work! He'd caught the wrong train, got off at a station he didn't recognize. Caught another train he *thought* was going back—and ended up in a place he'd never even heard of! He'd been lucky that time: he'd eventually made it home without getting lost again.

But...he wasn't the only one. At least he could take some comfort in that. There were others just like him. For example, the big man in Queen Street. How *can* one get lost in his own street, outside his own home?

And what of Mildred? Had she really run off, or was she simply...lost? Howard's hair stood on end. What if, right now, she was out there somewhere, trying to find her way back home? Trapped in a superstore? Lost around the corner? Marooned in the next street? Becalmed next door? Castaway in Kings Cross? *Verlorn* in Fulham? Shanghaied in Shepperton? Mislaid in Marble Arch? Confused in Crouch End? Adrift in Arsenal?

Lost!

Howard was hungry. His new idea was growing, spreading through his entire being, filling his mind and emptying his stomach. He had always been the same: excited, he got hungry. Most people are like that; it's why they sell food at cinemas, football matches, airports. Alter the metabolism, change the heartbeat, pulse, environment physical and mental, and the stomach always seeks to compensate. He wanted food. Then he might consider his idea some more, see where it led him. Just as long as it led him in a direction he recognized! Just as long as it didn't elude him utterly. Lose him.

It took him a while to find the kitchen, the fridge, the cooking fat, the frying pan, but eventually he fried and ate eggs and bacon. And while he munched, so his mind worked. Could it be—really be—that the entire world was losing its direction? Did anyone know where he was anymore?

Howard went to what he thought was the window and drew back the curtains, then stood for long moments looking into an alcove he had hoped would be the street outside. Jesus!—he couldn't even find his way round his own home anymore! Using the alcove as a landmark, he found his way to the window. Out there, the street—which he barely recognized. And no one out there, afraid to leave their homes, afraid that they wouldn't be able to find their way back.

Before the panic could set in again, he ran like a startled cockroach through the house, found the bathroom, the loo, the bedroom (that one was difficult) and finally made his way back to the living-room. But...he had also found rooms he didn't know—or rooms which hadn't seemed to know him—where he had been a stranger. In them he had been lost, or they had been lost around him.

Ridiculous! Idiotic! Or else...

...Maybe he was going mad?

No, no, *no*! That was silly. He felt so, well, sane!—didn't he? How could one reason like this if one were mad? One couldn't. Not possibly. Ill, yes—but not mad.

With a little effort he found the telephone, 'phoned his office. His boss, Mr. Jackson, worked late these days. Always. Howard knew Mr. Jackson would be there. And he was.

"Jackson?" the voice over the wire sounded utterly fatigued.

"Howard here, sir," said Howard, trying to sound calm. "Howard Pratt."

"Oh, yes, Howard," the voice was tinny, came from a thousand miles away. "Good evening. What can I do for you?"

I...sir, I won't be in tomorrow. I'm...not too well. I have to... to see...to see a doctor."

"Thank you for letting me know, Howard," said the voice from Mars.

"Yes," said Howard. But—

"—Howard, wait!"

"I'm waiting, sir."

"Where are you, Howard?"

"Why, I'm home, sir!"

After a long moment Howard heard a deep, deep sigh. "Home," Mr. Jackson whispered. Then he coughed and cleared his throat. "Home, yes—of course you're at home. Well, I'll see you when you get back, Howard." But he didn't put down the 'phone.

Howard waited again, then said: "Sir?"

"Yes?"

"It's late sir. Why don't *you* go home?"

A distant sob sounded. And: "Oh, I've tried, Howard. Believe me, I've tried." Then a click, and the dead 'phone humming in Howard's hand.

Howard went to bed, lay there in the dark, smoked a

cigarette—smoked ten of them—but he didn't sleep. He simply thought.

He thought about it all, about everything.

About a world which had lost its direction, its identity, its aim. An entire world, wandering. Lost.

If you can't beat 'em, Howard thought, join 'em. It's the only thing to do.

In the morning he put on his clothes, his overcoat, his hat, took up his umbrella (it was raining) and went out. He knew the risk, the danger, and welcomed it. At least he was part of it now, whatever it was. He was deep in it, not fumbling around on the perimeter.

At the end of the street, already wondering where he was, he looked back, grinned and nodded.

Lost.

Lost, yes!

A big man he knew from somewhere grabbed his shoulders, peered hopelessly into Howard's eyes. "Queen Street, mate!" he whispered. "Queen Street!"

"Sorry," said Howard. "I'm a stranger here myself..."

SNARKER'S SON

Oh yeah, yet another problem child – isn't he?

"All right, all right!" Sergeant Scott noisily submitted. "So you're lost. You're staying with your dad here in the city at a hotel—you were sightseeing and you got separated—I accept all that. But look, son, we've had lost kids in here before, often, and they didn't try on all this silly stuff about names and spellings and all!"

Sergeant Scott had known—had been instinctively "aware" all day—that this was going to be one of *those* shifts. Right up until ten minutes ago his intuition had seemed for once to have let him down. But now...

"It's true," the pallid, red-eyed nine-year old insisted, hysteria in his voice. "It's all true, everything I've said. This town *looks* like Mondon—but it's not! And...and before I came in here I passed a store called Woolworths—but it should have been 'Wolwords'!"

"All right, let's not start that again." The policeman put up quieting hands. "Now: you say you came down with your father from...from Sunderpool? That's in England?"

"No, I've *told* you," the kid started to cry again. "It's 'Eenland'!" We came down on holiday from Sunderpool by longcar, and—"

"Longcar?" Sergeant Scott cut in, frowning. "Is that some place on the north-east coast?"

"No, it's not a place! A longcar is...well, a *longcar*! Like a buzz but longer, and it goes on the longcar lanes. You know...?"

The boy looked as puzzled as Sergeant Scott, to say nothing of accusing.

"No, I don't know!" The policeman shook his head, trying to control his frown. "A 'buzz'?" Scott could feel the first twinges of one of his bilious headaches coming on, and so-decided to change the subject. "What does your father do, son? He's a science-fiction writer, eh?—And you're next in a long line?"

"Dad's a Snarker," the answer came quite spontaneously, without any visible attempt at deceit or even flippancy. In any case, the boy was obviously far too worried to be flippant. A "nut," Scott decided—but nevertheless a nut in trouble.

Now the kid had an inquisitive look on his face. "What's science-fiction?" he asked.

"Science-fiction," the big sergeant answered him with feeling, "is that part of a policeman's lot called 'desk-duty'— when crazy lost kids walk into the station in tears to mess up said policeman's life!"

His answer set the youngster off worse than before.

Sighing, Scott passed his handkerchief across the desk and stood up. He called out to a constable in an adjacent room:

"Hey, Bob, come and look after the desk until Sergeant Healey gets in, will you? He's due on duty in the next ten minutes or so. I'll take the kid and see if I can find his father. If I can't—well, I'll bring the boy back here and the job can go through the usual channels."

"All right, Sergeant, I'll watch the shop," the constable agreed as he came into the duty-room and took his place at the desk. "I've been listening to your conversation! Right rum 'un that," he grinned, nodding towards the tearful boy. "What an imagination!"

Imagination, yes. And yet Scott wasn't quite sure. There was "something in the air," a feeling of impending *strangeness*— hard to define.

"Come on, son," he said, shaking off his mood. "Let's go."

He took the boy's hand. "Let's see if we can find your dad. He's probably rushing about right now wondering what's become of you." He shook his head in feigned defeat and said:

"I don't know—ten o'clock at night, just going off duty—and you have to walk in on me."

"Ten o'clock—*already*?" The boy looked up into Scott's face with eyes wider and more frightened than ever. "Then we only have half an hour!

"Eh?" the policeman frowned again as they passed out into the London street (or was it "Mondon," Scott wondered with a mental grin he couldn't quite suppress). "Half an hour? What happens at half past ten, son? Do you turn into a pumpkin or something?" His humor was lost on his small charge.

"I mean the *lights!*" the boy answered, in what Scott took to be exasperation. "That's when the lights go out. At half past ten they put the lights out!"

"Oh? They do?" the sergeant had given up trying to penetrate the boy's fertile but decidedly warped imagination. "Why's that, I wonder?" (Let the kid ramble on; it was better than tears, at any rate.)

"Don't you know *anything*? the youngster seemed half-astonished, half-unbelieving, almost as if he thought Scott was pulling his leg.

"No," the sergeant returned, "I'm just a stupid copper! But come on—where did you give your father the slip? You said you passed Woolworths getting to the police station. Well, Woolworths is down this way, near the tube." He looked at the boy sharply in mistaken understanding. "You didn't get lost on the tube, did you? Lots of kids do when it's busy."

"The Tube?" Scott sensed that the youngster spoke the words in capitals—and yet it was only a whisper. He had to hold on tight as the boy strained away from him in something akin to horror. "No one goes down in the Tube anymore, except…" He shuddered.

"Yes?" Scott pressed, interested in this particular part of the boy's fantasy despite himself and his need, now, to have done with what would normally be a routine job. "Except who?"

"Not *who*," the boy told him, clutching at his hand again, tightly. "Not, who, but—"

"But?" again, patiently, Scott prompted him.

"Not who, but *what!*"

"Well, go on," said the sergeant, sighing, leading the way down the quiet, half-deserted street towards Woolworths. "*What*, er, goes down in the tube?

"Why, Tubers, of course!" Again there was astonishment in the youngster's voice, amazement at Scott's obvious deficiency in general knowledge. "Aren't you Mondoners *thick!*" It was a statement of fact, not a question.

"Right," said Scott, not bothering to pursue the matter further, seeing the pointlessness of questioning an idiot. "We've passed Woolworths—now where?

"Over there, I think, down that street, Yes!—that's where I lost my father—down there!"

"Come on," Scott said, leading the boy across the road, empty now of all but the occasional car, down into the entrance of the indicated street. In fact it was little more than an alley, dirty and unlighted. "What on earth were you doing down here in the first place?"

"We weren't down here," the youngster answered with a logic that made the sergeant's head spin. "We were in a bright street, with lots of lights. Then I felt a funny tingling feeling, and… and then I was here! I got frightened and ran."

At that moment, their footsteps echoing hollowly on the cobbles of the alley, the sergeant felt a weird vibration that began in his feet and traveled up his body to his head, causing a burst of bright, painfully bilious stars to flash across his vision—and simultaneously with this peculiar sensation the two turned a corner to emerge with startling abruptness into a much brighter side street.

"That was the tingling I told you about," the boy stated, almost unnecessarily.

Scott wasn't listening. He was looking behind him for the severed electric cable he felt sure must be lying there just inside the alley; for the weird sensation must surely have been caused by a sharp electric shock. But he couldn't see any cable. Nor could he see anything else that might have explained that tingling, buzzing, nerve-rasping sensation he had known. And for that matter, where was the entrance (or exit) from which he and the boy had just this minute emerged?

Where was the alley?

"Dad!" the kid yelled, suddenly tugging himself free to go racing off down the street.

Scott stood and watched., his head starting to throb and the street lights flaring garishly before his eyes. At the boy's cry a lone man had turned, started to run, and now Scott saw him sweep the lad up, hugging him wildly, intense and obvious relief showing in his face…

The policeman forgot the problem of the vanishing alley and walked up to them, hands behind his back in the approved fashion, smiling benignly. "Cute lad you've got there, sir—but I should curb his imagination if I were you. Why, he's been telling me a story fit to—"

Then the benign smile slid from his face. "*Here!*" he cried, his jaw dropping in astonishment.

But despite his exclamation, Scott was nevertheless left standing on his own. For without a word of thanks both man and boy had made off down the street, hands linked, running as if the devil himself was after them!

"Here!" the policeman called again, louder. "Hold on a bit…"

For a moment the pair stopped and turned, then the man glanced at this watch (reminding Scott curiously of the White Rabbit in *Alice in Wonderland*) before picking up the boy again and holding him close. Then: "Get off the streets!" he yelled back at Scott as he once more started to run. "Get off the streets, man!" White-faced, he glanced back and up at the street lights as he ran, and Scott saw absolute terror shining in his eyes. "It'll soon be half past ten!"

The policeman was still in the same position, his jaw hanging slack, some seconds later when the figure of the unknown man, still hugging the boy to him, vanished around a distant corner. Then he shrugged his shoulders and tried to pull himself together, setting his helmet more firmly on his aching head.

"Well I'll be—" He grinned nervously through the throb of his headache. "Snarker's son, indeed!"

Alone, now, Scott's feeling of impending *something* returned, and he noticed suddenly just how deserted the street was. He had never known London so quite before. Why, there wasn't a single soul in sight!

And a funny thing, but here he was, only a stone's throw from his station, where he'd worked for the last fifteen years of his life, and yet—damned if he could recognize the street! Well, he knew he'd brought the boy down a dark, cobbled alley from the right, and so...

He took the first street on the right, walking quickly down it until he hit another street he knew somewhat better—

Or did he?

Yes, yes, of course he did. The street was deserted now, quite empty, but just over there was good old...

Good old Wolwords!

Lights blazed and burst into multicolored sparks before Scott's bilious eyes. His mind spun wildly. He grabbed hold of a lamppost to steady himself and tried to think the thing out properly.

It must be a new building, that place—yes, that had to be the answer. He'd been doing a lot of desk-duties lately, after all. It was quite possible, what with all the new techniques, and the speed of modern building, that the store had been put up in just a few weeks.

The place didn't *look* any too new, though....

Scott's condition rapidly grew worse—understandably in the circumstances, he believed—but there was a tube station nearby. He decided to take a train home. He usually walked the mile or so to his flat, the exercise did him good; but tonight he would take a train, give himself a rest.

He went dizzily down one flight of steps, barely noticing the absence of posters and the unkempt, dirty condition of the underground. Then, as he turned a corner, he came face-to-face with a strange legend, sprawling in red paint across the tiled wall:

ROT THE TUBERS!

Deep creases furrowed the sergeant's forehead as he walked on, his footsteps ringing hollowly in the grimy, empty corridors, but his headache just wouldn't let him think clearly.

Tubers, indeed! What the hell—Tubers…?

Down another flight of steps he went, to the deserted ticket booths, where he paused to stare in disbelief at the naked walls of the place and the dirt- and refuse-littered floor. For the first time he really saw the *condition* of the place. What happened here? Where was everyone?

From beyond the turnstiles he heard the rumble of a distant train and the spell lifted a little. He hurried forward then, past the empty booths and through the unguarded turnstiles, dizzily down one more flight of concrete steps, under an arch and out onto an empty platform. Not even a drunk or a tramp shared the place with him. The neons flared hideously, and he put out a hand against the naked wall for support.

Again, through the blinding flashes of light in his head, he noticed the absence of posters; the employment agencies, the pretty girls in lingerie, the film and play adverts, spectacular films and *avant-garde* productions—where in the hell were they all?

Then, as for the first time he truly felt upon his spine the chill fingers of a slithering horror, there came the rumble and blast of air that announced the imminent arrival of a train—and he smelled the rushing reek of that which most certainly was *not* a train!

Even as he staggered to and fro on the unkempt platform, reeling under the fetid blast that engulfed him, the Tuber rushed from out its black hole—a *Thing* of crimson viscosity and rhythmically flickering cilia.

Sergeant Scott gave a wild shriek as a rushing feeler swept him from the platform and into the soft, hurtling plasticity of the thing—another shriek as he was whisked away into the deep tunnel and down into the bowels of the earth. And seconds later the minute hand of the clock above the empty, shuddering platform clicked down into the vertical position.

Ten-thirty: and all over Mondon—indeed throughout the length and breadth of Eenland—the lights went out…

WHAT DARK GOD?

"Summanus—whatever power he may be...."—*Ovid's Fasti*
Train wrecks are more than enough – without passengers!

The Tuscan Rituals? Now where had I heard of such a book or books before? Certainly very rare.... Copy in the British Museum? Perhaps! Then what on earth were *these* fellows doing with a copy? And such a strange bunch of blokes at that.

Only a few minutes earlier I had boarded the train at Bengham. It was quite crowded for a night train and the boozy, garrulous, and vociferous "Jock" who had boarded it directly in front of me had been much upset by the fact that all the compartments seemed to be fully occupied.

"Och, they bleddy British trains," he had drunkenly grumbled, "either a'wiz emp'y or a'wiz fool. No orgynization whatsayever—ye no agree, ye Sassenach?" He had elbowed me in the ribs as we swayed together down the dim corridor.

"Er, yes," I had answered. "Quite so!"

Neither of us carried cases and as we stumbled along, searching for vacant seats in the gloomy compartments, Jock suddenly stopped short.

"Noo what in hell's this—will ye look here? A compartment wi' the bleddy blinds doon. Prob'ly a young laddie an' lassie in there wi' six emp'y seats. Privacy be damned. Ah'm no standin' oot here while there's a seat in there..."

The door had proved to be locked—on the inside—but that had not deterred the "bonnie Scot" for a moment. He had banged insistently upon the wooden frame of the door until it was carefully, tentatively opened a few inches; then he had stuck his foot in the gap and put his shoulder to the frame, forcing the door fully open.

"No, no…!" The scrawny, pale, pinstripe-jacketed man who stood blocking the entrance protested. "You can't come in—this compartment is reserved!"

"Is that so, noo? Well, if ye'll kindly show me the reserved notice," Jock had paused to tap significantly upon the naked glass of the door with a belligerent fingernail, "Ah'll bother ye no more—meanwhile, though, if ye'll hold ye're blether, *Ah'd appreciate a bleddy seat!*"

"No, no…!" The scrawny man had started to protest again, only to be quickly cut off by a terse command from behind him: "Let them in!"

I shook my head and pinched my nose, blowing heavily and puffing out my cheeks to clear my ears. For the voice from within the dimly-lit compartment had sounded hollow, unnatural. Possibly the train had started to pass through a tunnel, an occurrence which never fails to give me trouble with my ears. I glanced out of the exterior corridor window and saw immediately that I was wrong; far off on the dark horizon I could see the red glare of coke-oven fires. Anyway, whatever the effect had been which had given that voice its momentarily peculiar—resonance?—it had obviously passed, for Jock's voice sounded perfectly normal as he said: "Noo tha's *better*; excuse a body, will ye?" He shouldered the dubious-looking man in the doorway to one side and slid clumsily into a seat alongside a second stranger. As I joined them in the compartment, sliding the door shut behind me, I saw that there were four strangers in all, six people including Jock and myself; we just made comfortable use of the eight seats which faced inwards in two sets of four.

I have always been a comparatively shy person so it was only the vaguest of perfunctory glances which I gave to each of the three new faces before I settled back and took out the pocketbook I had picked up earlier in the day in London.

Those merest of glances, however, were quite sufficient to put me off my book and to tell me that the three friends of the pinstripe-jacketed man appeared the very strangest of travelling companions—especially the extremely tall and thin member of the three, sitting stiffly in his seat beside Jock. The other two answered to approximately the same description as Pin-Stripe—as I was beginning mentally to tag him—except that one of them wore a thin moustache; but that fourth one, the tall one, was something else again.

Within the brief duration of the glance I had given him I had seen that, remarkable though the rest of his features were, his mouth appeared decidedly odd—almost as if it had been painted onto his face—the merest thin red line, without a trace of puckering or any other depression to show that there was a hole there at all. His ears were thick and blunt and his eyebrows were bushy over the most penetrating eyes it has ever been my unhappy lot to find staring at me. Possibly that was the reason I had glanced so quickly away; the fact that when I had looked at him I had found *him* staring at *me*—and his face had been totally devoid of any expression whatsoever. *Fairies?* The nasty thought had flashed through my mind unbidden; nonetheless, that would explain why the door had been locked.

Suddenly Pin-Stripe—seated next to me and directly opposite Funny-Mouth—gave a start, and, as I glanced up from my book, I saw that the two of them were staring directly into each other's eyes.

"*Tell them...*" Funny-Mouth said, though I was sure his strange lips had not moved a fraction, and again his voice had seemed distorted, as though his words passed through weirdly angled corridors before reaching my ears.

"It's, er—almost midnight," informed Pin-Stripe, grinning sickly first at Jock and then at me.

"Aye," said Jock sarcastically, "it happens every nicht aboot this time…. Ye're very observant."

"Yes," said Pin-Stripe, choosing to ignore the jibe, "as you say—but the point I wish to make is that we three, er, that is, we *four*," he corrected himself, indicating his companions with a nod of his head, "are members of a little-known, er, religious sect. We have a ceremony to perform and would appreciate it if you two gentlemen would remain quiet during the proceedings…."

I heard him out and nodded my head in understanding and

agreement—I am a tolerant person—but Jock was of a different mind.

"Sect?" he said sharply. "Ceremony?" He shook his head in disgust. "Well; Ah'm a member o' the Church o' Scotland and Ah'll tell ye noo—Ah'll hae no truck wi' bleddy heathen *ceremonies!*"

Funny-Mouth had been sitting ramrod straight, saying not a word, doing nothing, but now he turned to look at Jock, his eyes narrowing to mere slits; above them, his eyebrows meeting in a black frown of disapproval.

"Er, perhaps it would be better," said Pin-Stripe hastily, leaning across the narrow aisle towards Funny-Mouth as he noticed the change in that person's attitude, "if they, er, *went to sleep?*"

This preposterous statement or question, which caused Jock to peer at its author in blank amazement and me to wonder what on earth he was babbling about, was directed at Funny-Mouth who, without taking his eyes off Jock's outraged face, nodded in agreement.

I do not know what happened then—it was as if I had been suddenly *unplugged*—I was asleep, yet not asleep—in a trance-like condition full of strange impressions and mind-pictures—abounding in unpleasant and realistic sensations, with dimly-recollected snatches of previously absorbed information floating up to the surface of my conscious mind, correlating themselves with the strange people in the railway compartment with me.

And in that dream-like state my brain was still very active; possibly *fully* active. All my senses were still working; I could hear the clatter of the wheels and smell the acrid tang of burnt tobacco from the compartment's ashtrays. I saw Moustache produce a folding table from the rack above his head—saw him open it and set it up in the aisle, between Funny-Mouth and himself on their side and Pin-Stripe and his companion on my side—saw the designs upon it, designs suggestive of the more exotic work of Chandler Davies, and wondered at their purpose. My head must have fallen back until it rested in the corner of the gently rocking compartment, for I saw all these things without having to move my eyes; indeed, I doubt very much if I *could* have moved my eyes and do not remember making any attempt to do so.

I saw that book—a queerly-bound volume bearing its title, *The Tuscan Rituals*, in archaic, burnt-in lettering on its thick spine—produced by Pin-Stripe and opened reverently to lie on that ritualistic table, displayed so that all but Funny-Mouth, Jock, and I could make out its characters. But Funny-Mouth did not seem in the least bit interested in the proceedings. He gave me the impression that he had seen it all before, and many times.

Knowing I was dreaming—or was I?—I pondered that title, *The Tuscan Rituals*. Now where had I heard of such a book or books before? The *feel* of it echoed back into my subconscious, telling me I recognized that title—but in what connection?

I could see Jock, too, on the fixed border of my sphere of vision, lying with his head lolling towards Funny-Mouth—in a trance similar to my own, I imagined—eyes staring at the drawn blinds on the compartment windows. I saw the lips of Pin-Stripe, out of the corner of my right eye, and those of Moustache, moving in almost perfect rhythm, and imagined those of Other—as I had named the fourth who was completely out of my periphery of vision—doing the same, and heard the low and intricate liturgy which they were chanting in unison.

Liturgy? Tuscan rituals?...Now what dark "God" was this they worshipped? And what had made *that* thought spring to my dreaming or hypnotized mind? And what was Moustache doing now?

He had a bag and was taking things from it, laying them delicately on the ceremonial table. Three items in all; in one corner of the table, that nearest Funny-Mouth. Round cakes of wheat-bread in the shape of wheels with ribbed spokes. Now who had written about offerings of wheel-shaped cakes of...?

Festus? Yes, *Festus*—but, again, in what connection?

Then I heard it. A *name*: chanted by the three worshippers, but not by Funny-Mouth who still sat aloofly upright.

"Summanus, Summanus, Summanus...." they chanted; and suddenly, it all clicked into place.

Summanus! Of whom Martianus Capella had written as

being The Lord of Hell…. Oh, I remembered now. It was Pliny who, in his *Natural History*, mentioned the dreaded *Tuscan Rituals*, 'books containing the Liturgy of Summanus….'" Of course; Summanus—Monarch of Night—the Terror that Walketh in Darkness. Summanus, whose worshippers were so few and whose cult was surrounded with such mystery, fear, and secrecy that according to St Augustine even the most curious enquirer could discover no particular of it.

So Funny-Mouth, who stood so aloof to the ceremony in which the others were participating, must be a priest of the cult.

Though my eyes were fixed—my centre of vision being a picture, one of three, on the compartment wall just above Moustache's head—I could still clearly see Funny-Mouth's face and, as a blur to the left of my periphery, that of Jock.

The liturgy had come to an end with the calling of the "God's" name and the offering of bread. For the first time Funny-Mouth seemed to be taking an interest. He turned his head to look at the table and just as I was certain that he was going to reach out and take the bread-cakes the train lurched and Jock slid sideways in his seat, his face coming into clearer perspective as it came to rest about halfway down Funny-Mouth's upper right arm. Funny-Mouth's head snapped round in a blur of hate. *Hate*, livid and pure, shone from those cold eyes, was reflected by the bristling eyebrows and tightening features; only the strange, painted-on mouth remained sterile of emotion. But he made no effort to move Jock's head.

It was not until later that I found out what happened then. Mercifully my eyes could not take in the whole of the compartment—or what was happening in it. I only knew that Jock's face, little more than an outline with darker, shaded areas defining the eyes, nose, and mouth at the lower rim of my fixed '"picture," became suddenly contorted; twisted somehow, as though by some great emotion or pain. He said nothing, unable to break out of that damnable trance, but his eyes bulged horribly and his features writhed. If only I could have taken my eyes off him, or closed them even, to shut out the picture of his face writhing and Funny-Mouth staring at him so terribly. Then I noticed the change in Funny-Mouth. He had been a chalky-grey colour before; we all had, in the weak glow from the alternately brightening and dimming compartment ceiling light. Now he seemed to be *flushed*; pinkish waves of unnatural colour were suffusing his outré features and his red-slit mouth was fading into the deepening blush of his face. It almost looked as though.... *My God! He did not have a mouth!* With that unnatural reddening of his features the painted slit had vanished completely; his face was *blank* beneath the eyes and nose.

What a God-awful dream. I knew it must be a dream now— it *had* to be a dream—such things do not happen in real life. Dimly I was aware of Moustache putting the bread-cakes away and folding the queer table. I could feel the rhythm of the train slowing down. We must be coming into Grenloe. Jock's face was absolutely convulsed now. A white, twitching, jerking, bulge-eyed blur of hideous motion which grew paler as quickly as that of Funny-Mouth—if that name applied now—reddened. Suddenly Jock's face stopped its jerking. His mouth lolled open and his eyes slowly closed. He slid out of my circle of vision towards the floor.

The train was moving much slower and the wheels were clacking over those groups of crisscrossing rails which always warn one that a train is approaching a station or depot. Funny-Mouth had turned his monstrous, nightmare face towards me. He leaned across the aisle, closing the distance between us. I mentally screamed, physically incapable of the act, and strained with every fibre of my being to break from the trance which I suddenly knew beyond any doubting *was not a dream and never had been!*

The train ground to a shuddering halt with a wheeze of steam and a squeal of brakes. Outside in the night the station-master was yelling instructions to a porter on the unseen platform. As the train stopped, Funny-Mouth was jerked momentarily back, away from me, and before he could bring his face close to mine again Moustache was speaking to him.

"There's no time, Master—this is our stop!" Funny-Mouth hovered over me a moment longer, seemingly undecided, then he pulled away. The others filed past him out into the corridor while he stood, tall and eerie, just within the doorway. Then he lifted his right hand and snapped his fingers.

I could move. I blinked my eyes rapidly and shook myself, sitting up straight, feeling the pain of the cramp between my shoulder-blades.

"I say…" I began.

"*Quiet!*" ordered that echoing voice from unknown spaces—and of course, his painted, false mouth never moved. I was right; I had been hypnotized, not dreaming at all. That false mouth—Walker in Darkness—Monarch of Night—Lord of Hell—the Liturgy to Summanus!

I opened my mouth in amazement and horror, but before I could utter more than one word—"*Summanus* "—*something happened!*

His waistcoat slid to one side near the bottom and a long, white, tapering tentacle with a blood-red tip slid into view! That tip hovered, snake-like, for a moment over my petrified face— and then struck. As if someone had taken a razor to it, my face opened up and the blood began to gush. I fell to my knees in shock, too terrified even to yell out, automatically reaching for my handkerchief; and when next I coweringly looked up, Funny-Mouth had gone.

Instead of seeing him—*It*—I found myself staring, from where I kneeled dabbing uselessly at my face, into the slack features of the sleeping Jock.

Sleeping?

I began to scream. Even as the train started to pull out of the station I was screaming. When no one answered my cries, I managed to pull the communication-cord. Then, until they came to find out what was wrong, I went right on screaming. Not because of my face—*because of Jock!*

A jagged, bloody, two-inch hole led clean through his jacket and shirt and into his left side—the side which had been closest to…to that *thing—and there was not a drop of blood in his whole, limp body.* He simply lay there—half on, half off the seat—victim of "a bleddy heathen ceremony"—substituted for the bread-cakes simply because the train had chosen an inopportune moment to lurch—a sacrifice to Summanus!

THE STRANGE YEARS

Did you see them coming? Lumley did, twenty years earlier!

He was stretched out face-down on the beach at the foot of a small dune, his face turned just a little to one side. The summer sun was beating down on him, and the needle tips of a clump of beach-grass blades at the top of the dune were almost but not quite audibly vibrating in the breeze off the sea. In the shade of the dune, however, all was calm, with not even a seagull's mournful cry to break in on the lulling *hush, hush* of waves from far down the beach.

It would be nice, he thought, to run down the beach and splash in the sea, and come back dripping salt water and tasting it on his lips, and for the very briefest of moments be a small boy again in a world with a future. But the sun beat down from a blue sky and his limbs were leaden, and a great drowsiness was upon him.

Then...a disturbance. Blown on the breeze to climb the far side of the dune, flapping like a bird with broken wings, a slim book—a child's exercise book, with tables of weights and measures on the back—flopped down exhausted in the sand before his eyes. Disinterested, he found strength to push it away; but as his fingers touched it so its cover blew open to reveal pages written in a neat if shaky adult longhand.

He had nothing else to do, and so began to read....

When did it begin? Where? How? Why?

The Martians, we might have expected (writers had been

frightening us long enough with their tales of invasions from outer space,) and certainly there have been enough of threats from foreign "comrades" across the water. But this?

Any ordinary sort of plague, we would survive. We always have in the past. And as for war: Christ!—when has there *not* been a war going on somewhere? They've irradiated us in Japan, defoliated us in Vietnam, smothered us in DDT wherever we were arable, and poured poison into us where we once flowed sweet and clean—and we always bounced right back.

Fire and flood—even nuclear fire and festering effluent—have not appreciably stopped us. For "they" read "We," Man, and for "us" read "the world," this Earth which once was ours. Yes, there have been weird times, strange years, but never a one as strange as now.

A penance? The ultimate penance? Or has Old Ma Nature finally decided to give us a hand? Perhaps She has stood off, watching us try our damnedest for so damned long to exterminate ourselves, and now She's sick to death of the whole damned scene. "OK," She says, "have it your way." And She gives the nod to Her Brother, the Old Boy with the scythe. And He sighs and steps forward, and—

And it *is* a plague, of sorts; and certainly it's a DOOM; and a fire that rages across the world to devour all life...or will that come later? A cleansing flame, from which Life's bright phoenix just might rise again? For after all there will always be the sea. And how many ages this time before something gets left by the tide, grows lungs, jumps up on its feet and walks...and reaches for a club?

When did it begin?

I remember an Irish stoker who came into a bar dirty and drunk. His sleeves were rolled up and he scratched at hairy arms. I thought it was the heat. "Hot? Damned right, sur," he said, "an' hotter by far down below—an' lousy!" He unrolled a newspaper on the bar and brushed vigorously at his matted forearm. Things fell onto the newsprint and moved, slowly. He popped them with a cigarette. "Crabs, sur!" he cried. "An' Christ!—they suck like crazy!"

When?

There have always been strange years—plague years, drought years, war and wonder years—so it's difficult to pin it down. But the last hundred…well, they have been really *strange*. When, *exactly*? Who can say? But let's give it a shot. Let's start with the 70s—say, '76?—yes, as early as all that. The drought.

There was so little water in the Thames that they said the river was running backwards. The militants blamed the Soviets. New laws were introduced to conserve water. People were taken to court for watering flowers. Some idiot calculated that a pound of excreta could be satisfactorily washed away with six pints of water, and people put bricks in their WC cisterns. Someone else said you could bathe comfortably in four inches of water, and if you didn't use soap the resultant mud could be thrown on the garden. The thing snowballed into a national campaign to 'Save It!'—and in October the skies were still cloudless, the earth parched, and imported rainmakers danced and pounded their tom-toms at Stonehenge. Forest and heath fires were daily occurrences and reservoirs became dustbowls. Sun-worshippers drank Coke and turned very brown…

And finally it rained, and it rained, and it rained. Widespread flooding, rivers bursting their banks, gardens (deprived all summer) inundated and washed away. Millions of tons of water, and little more than a couple of ounces of crap to be disposed of. A strange year, '76. And just about every year since, come to think.

'89, and stories leak out of the Ukraine of fifty thousand square miles turned brown and utterly barren in the space of a single week. Since then the spread has been very slow, but it hasn't stopped. The Russians blamed "us" and we accused "them" of testing a secret weapon.

'80 to '90, and oil tankers sinking or grounding themselves left, right and center. Miles-long oil slicks and chemicals jettisoned at sea, and whales washed up on the beaches while the Japanese continued to slaughter dolphins. Another drought, this time in Australia and a plague of mice to boot. Some Aussie commentating that "The poor 'roos are dyin' in their thousands—and a few aboes, too…" And great green swarms of aphids and skies bright with ladybirds.

Plague years, yes: lots of plagues, in fact. We were being warned, you see?

And between times…well let's not forget '84! Ah—1984! Good old George!

He was wrong, of course, for it wasn't Big Brother at all. It was Big Sister—Ma Nature Herself. And true, She waited a little while longer than George had forecast. But finally…well finally She really did go off the rails. Half of India eaten by locusts, and all Africa down with a mutant strain of beriberi. Then came the year of the poisoned potatoes and sinistral periwinkles, the year it rained frogs over wide areas of France, and the year the cane-pest propelled sugar beet right up to the top of the crops.

And then…not only Ma Nature but Technology, too, coming unstuck. The Lake District chemically polluted, and permanently; nuclear power stations at Lock Torr on one side of the Atlantic and Long Island on the other melting down simultaneously; the Americans bringing back a "bug" from Mars (see, even a *real* Martian invasion); oil discovered in the Mediterranean, and new fast-drilling techniques cracking the ocean floor and allowing it to leak and leak and leak…even Red Adair would have been shaking his head in dismay! (How do you plug a leak a thousand fathoms deep and fifty miles long?) And that jewel of the oceans turning black, and Cyprus a great white tombstone in a graveyard of pitch. "Aphrodite Rising from the High-Grade."

Then for a period…nothing! And that was strange, too, and even more frightening, because it was so damned quiet! The lull before the storm, so to speak. But in just a handful more of years:

It was the American space-bug, leaping to Australia and New Zealand and giving both places a monstrous malaise. No one doing any real work; cattle and sheep dead in their millions; entire cities and town burning down because nobody bothered to call out the fire services—or they didn't bother to come…. And all the world's beaches strewn with a countless myriad of great dead octopuses, a new species (or a mutant strain) with three rows of suckers to each tentacle; and their stink utterly unbearable as they rotted. A plague of huge fat seagulls—the octopuses, of course—and all the major volcanoes erupting in unison. Meteoric debris making massive holes in the ionosphere...a new killer cancer caused by sunburn...the common cold cured!...And uncommon leprosy spreading like wildfire throughout the Western World.

Until finally...

Well, that was "When." It was also, I fancy, "Where" and "How!" As to "Why"...but here I can only offer a mental shrug. I'm tired, probably hungry. I have some sort of lethargy—the space-bug, I suppose—and I reckon it won't be long now.

I had hoped that getting this down on paper might keep me active, mentally if not physically active. But...

"Why?"

Well, I think I've answered that one, too:

Ma Nature strikes back, full force! Get rid of the human vermin, She thinks. They're lousing up my planet! And maybe *that's* what gave Her the idea. If fire and flood and disease and disaster and war couldn't do the trick, what else *could* She do?

They advise you to fight fire with fire, don't they? So why not vermin with vermin?

They appeared almost overnight, five times larger than their immediate progenitors and growing bigger with each successive hatching; but unlike the new octopus they didn't die; and their incubation period was less than a month. The super-lice: all Man's little body parasites—all of his tiny, personal vampires—and growing so rapidly into things as big as your fists. Leaping things, flying things, walking sideways things. To quote a certain Irishman: "An' Christ—they suck like crazy!"

They've sucked, all right. They've sucked the world to death. They have new protections—new immunities and near-invulnerability—to go with their new size and strength. The meek inheriting the Earth? Stamp on them and they scurry away. Spray them with lethal chemicals and they bathe in them. Feed them DDT and they develop a taste for it. "An' Christ—they suck like crazy!"

And the whole world down with the creeping, sleeping sickness. We didn't even *want* to fight them! They're like vampires, and always learning new tricks. Like camouflage:

clinging to walls above doors, they can look like bricks or tiles—
until you try to go through the door...

And their bite acts like a sort of LSD. Brings on mild
hallucinations, a feeling of well-being, a kind of euphoria. In the
cities, amongst the young, huge gangs of 'bug-people!' My God!

They use animals, too; dogs and cats—as mounts, to get
them about when they're bloated. Oh, they kill these slaves
eventually, but they know how to use them first. Dogs can dig
under walls and fences; cats can climb and squeeze through
tiny openings; crows and other large birds can fly down on top
of things and into places...

Me, I was lucky—if you can call it that. A bachelor, two dogs,
a parakeet and an outdoor aviary; my bungalow entirely netted
in; fine wire netting, with trees, trellises and vines. And best
of all, I was situated on a wild stretch of the coast, away from
mankind's great masses. But even so, it was only a matter of time.

They came, found me, sat outside my house, outside the wire
and the walls, and they waited. They found ways in. Dogs dug
holes for them, seagulls tore at the mesh overhead. Frantically, I
would trap, pour petrol, burn, listen to them pop! But I couldn't
stay awake for ever. One by one they got the birds, leaving little
empty bodies and bunches of feathers. And my dogs, Bill and
Ben, which I had to shoot and burn. And this morning when I
woke up, Peter parakeet...

So, there's at least one of them, probably two or three, here in
the room with me right now. Hiding, waiting for night. Waiting
for me to go to sleep. I've looked for them, of course, but—

Chameleons, they fit perfectly into any background. When I
move, they move. And they imitate perfectly...but they do make
mistakes. A moment ago I had two hairbrushes, identical, and
I've only ever had one. Can you imagine brushing your hair
with something like *that*? And what the hell would I want with
three fluffy slippers? A left, a right—and a center?

...I can see the beach from my window. And half a mile
away, on the point, there's Carter's grocery. Not a crust in the
kitchen. Dare I chance it? Do I want to? Let's see, now. Biscuits,
coffee, powdered milk, canned beans, potatoes—no, strike the
potatoes! But a sack of carrots...?

The man on the beach grinned mirthlessly, white lips drawing back from his teeth and freezing there. A year ago he would have expected to read such in a book of horror fiction. But not now. Not when it was written in his own hand.

The breeze changed direction, blew on him, and the sand began to drift against his side. It blew in his eyes, glazed now and lifeless. The shadows lengthened as the sun started to dip down behind the dunes. His body grew cold, colder.

Three hairy sacks with pincer feet, big as footballs and heavy with his blood, crawled slowly away from him along the beach....

THE MAN WHO SAW NO SPIDERS

You thought they wanted to?

"He what?" asked Bleaker, Conway's neighbour, incredulously.

Conway smiled at his friend's astounded expression, then repeated himself, adding: "It's quite genuine, I assure you, Jerry. He won't admit of spiders. They don't exist for him."

"Then of course he's a madman," Bleaker shrugged. "I mean, it's like someone saying he doesn't believe in mushrooms…isn't it?"

"Not at all," Conway answered. "The man who says he doesn't believe in mushrooms at least admits of their theory—by the very act of naming them—if you see what I mean?"

"Frankly, no," Bleaker shook his head, reaching for his drink. He lived only a short walk away from Conway, along a beautifully wooded path, set back half a mile from the main road that wound out from the nearby town and over the hills northward. The area was lonely but lovely and a handful of well-to-do families had their homes on the edge of the woods that stretched away to the hills. Bleaker and Conway had built comparatively close together, hence they were "neighbours," even though their houses stood almost a quarter-mile apart.

"OK, Jerry, look at it this way," Conway persisted. "If I say I don't believe in God, then there's not a great deal you can do to convince me that God does indeed exist, is there? No I'm not trying to be offensive, I assure you. I could just as easily have made it Father Christmas or Easter Bunny. However, while I don't admit of a God, I can readily enough understand others who do believe. I know what they are on about; I understand the theory of it."

"Yes, but—" Bleaker began, wishing that the girls would come on out of Conway's kitchen and get him off his psychiatric hobbyhorse.

"—But suppose I refuse to accept something as tangible as a good old fashioned English mushroom. What then?"

"Why, then I bring you one, Paul. I let you touch it, smell it, eat the bloody thing! I show you the word in an encyclopaedia with a picture of the real thing alongside. I get out a dictionary and spell it out for you: m-u-s-h-r-o-o-m...! I take you into town, the market on a Friday, where I buy you a pound of them. You can't escape them, they're there. Mushrooms *are*—you have to accept them." He sat back, smiling at his own cleverness.

"Good!" said Conway, successful psychiatrist written all over his face. "Now then, assume that when you bring me the mushroom I ignore it. Assume that my senses won't, *can't* recognize it. Assume that when I look at your dictionary I see 'mush' above and 'mushiness' below, but no 'mushroom' in between. That I don't even hear you when you say the word 'mushroom.' That I wonder why you're making funny faces when you spell the word out for me. What then?"

"Then you're a nut, pure and simple."

"Oh? And suppose that in every other instance I am a perfectly normal human being. An upstanding member of the community. A happily married man with no problems worth mentioning. In short, assume that in every way save one it's clearly demonstrable that I am *not* a nut. How about that?"

Bleaker frowned. "Hmm...! Could you possibly have some new, weird, exotic disease? Shall we call it, say, 'fungitis?' Even then, though, it has to be a disease of the mind. However harmless you are, you still have to be a nut."

Conway looked disappointed. "Yes, well the man we're talking about is not a nut. He's Thomas Waterford, gamekeeper for Lord Daventry at The Lodge. And with him it's not mushrooms but spiders. He doesn't believe in them, can't see them, he might as well never have heard of them. And from what I've seen of him, he'll never hear of them again."

"He's a nut," Bleaker insisted, without emphasis.

"He's as sane as you or I," Conway denied. "I've used every trick in the psychiatric book to test his sanity and I'm certain of it."

"So what caused it then?" Bleaker demanded to know. "Has he always been this way?"

"Ah! Good question. No, he hasn't always been this way; I was lucky to get onto him so quickly. It started a week ago yesterday, on a Saturday morning. Rather it started on the Friday, when his wife asked him to clean all the cobwebs and spiders out of the cellar of the gatehouse where they live. She hates spiders, you see. Yes, that was on the Friday. He told her he was busy, said that Lord Daventry was worried about poachers and he'd be out in the woods for most of the night, but that he'd clean out the spiders in the morning. He *believed* in spiders then, you see? But when she reminded him on the Saturday he ignored her. And when she took him down into the cellar to see how badly infested the place was, he—"

"He couldn't see the spiders?"

"Right! At first she thought he was kidding her on, but later she started to worry about it. On Monday she told Lord Daventry about it and he had a go at old Thomas. Then he contacted me. It seemed such an interesting case that I took it on gratis, as a favour. I drove over the hills to The Lodge that same afternoon…" He paused.

Interested despite himself, Bleaker prompted him: "And?"

"Jerry, it's like nothing I ever dealt with before. For the last five or six days spiders have had no place whatsoever in Thomas Waterford's life. Here, listen to this tape. I recorded it on Wednesday morning, five days after the thing began." He went over to his tape-recorder and pressed a button, listening as snatches of speeded-up conversation babbled forth until he found the spot he was looking for. A second button slowed the tape down and the recorded conversation became audible:

"*Well, we really don't seem to be getting anywhere, do we, Thomas?*"

"*P'raps we would, sir, if I knew what you was after. I've plenty of work on at The Lodge, and—*"

"But Lord Daventry said you'd be only too happy to help me out, Thomas."

"'Course, sir, but we don't seem to be doing much really, do we? I mean—wot am I 'ere for?"

"Spiders, Thomas!"

(Silence.)

"Why are you afraid of them?"

"Afraid of wot, sir?"

"Creepy-crawlies."

"Wot, bugs and beetles and flies, sir? I hain't scared of 'em sir! Wotever made you think that?"

"No, I meant spiders, Thomas. Hairy-legged web-spinners!"

"I mean, I sees bugs every day in the woods, I do, and—"

"And birds?"

"Lots of 'em."

"And trees?"

"'Ere, you're 'aving me on!"

"And—spiders?"

"'Course I sees trees! The 'ole bleedin' forest's full of 'em!"

Conway speeded the tape up at this point, and while it crackled and blustered on he said to Bleaker, "Listen to this next bit. This was the next day, Thursday. I had some rough drawings for Thomas to look at…"

He slowed the tape down and after a few seconds Bleaker heard the following:

"Just have a look at this, Thomas will you? What do you reckon that is?"

"Bird, sir. Thrush, I'd say, but not a very good drawing."

"And this one?"

"An eft. Newt, you'd call it, but I've always called 'em efts."

"And this?"

"A tree, probably a hoak—but wot's the point of all—"

"And—this?"

"Blank, sir. A blank piece of paper!"

(Pause, then a cough from Conway.)

"And, how about, er, this?"

"A bleedin' happle, sir!"

"Yes, but what's on the apple?"

"Eh? Why, a stalk, and a leaf."

"And?...What's this thing here, staring at you?"

"'Ere! You're 'aving me on again, hain't you? There's nothin' there 'cept your finger, sir!..."

Conway switched the tape-recorder off. He looked at Bleaker and said, "Both the 'blank' and the thing on the apple were—"

"Spiders?"

Conway nodded.

At that point the women came in from the kitchen carrying plated salads. "Spiders!" exclaimed Dorothy, Conway's wife, in disgust. She turned to Bleaker. "Don't tell me he's going on about old Tom Waterford again? I've had to listen to nothing else for a week!"

"But this sounds *so* interesting," said Bleaker's wife Andrea. "What's it all about? One of your cases, Paul?"

Dorothy held up her hand and took charge of the situation before it could get out of hand. "No you don't, Paul, not tonight. You've got Jerry here bored stiff. And anyway, I've told you what the answer is."

"Oh?" Bleaker looked at her. "What do you reckon then, Dorothy?"

She held up a finger and shushed them, looking very serious. "Flying saucers!" she said.

They all laughed.

"Oh, it's not so funny," she cautioned, unable to avoid giggling, despite her semi-serious expression. "It was just before old Tom went funny that the light was seen over the hills."

"A light?" Andrea repeated, completely out of her depth.

"Yes, a queer light, over the hills near Lord Daventry's place," Dorothy said. "Myself, I reckon the Martians got old Tom!" And again they all laughed; but Dorothy laughed loudest for she'd succeeded in changing the subject, which was all she had wanted to do...

The "lights" were seen again much later that same night, this time from the other side of the hills. Lord Daventry, sitting in his study, caught the bluish flash out of the corner of his eye as he sat studying some papers. Looking out of his window, away over the hills he saw a beam of light like a solid bar striking from heaven to the earth. It lasted for just a second, then was gone, but it reminded him of similar lights he had seen over a week ago. That had been about the time that old Tom started his queer business.

Thinking about his gamekeeper made the peer suddenly wonder how Conway was getting on with the case. Lord Daventry knew that the psychiatrist had spent a fair amount of time with Thomas.

Well, Conway usually worked late, didn't he? There was no reason why he shouldn't call the man up and find out how things stood. They were, after all, old friends of sorts. Perhaps he'd also ask if Conway had seen the light. He thought about it for a few minutes more, then picked up his telephone and dialled Conway's number.

He heard the answering *brrp, brrp, brrp,* from the other end, then the distant telephone was lifted from its cradle in Conway's study. "Conway? Said the Lord. "I hope I've not got you out of bed?"

"Not at all," Conway's voice came back, promptly and clearly. "I was doing a bit of work. Had a drink with some friends earlier but they're long gone. Dorothy's in bed."

"Good. I just wondered if you'd seen that peculiar light? I saw it a minute or so ago from my window. Seemed to shine down pretty close to your place. Funny sort of thing..."

Conway didn't answer. He was staring out of his own window. Out there, just beyond the dense copse at the foot of the garden, emitting a pulsing sort of auroral radiance whose like he had never in his life seen before, the bluish dome of an alien vessel showed like an obscene blister against the background of nighted hills. Closer to the house, looking at Conway where he stood staring out of the window, something loomed on stilt-like legs—something huge, hairy and hideously ugly beyond nightmare—something much more monstrously alien than the spacecraft which had brought it here.

It was, of sorts, a spider—but already Conway was beginning to forget that there were such things.

The bushes at the side of the house, from which even now a smaller spider emerged, swaying almost mechanically into view; the garden and copse and blister of strange light beyond; the dark backdrop of hills and roof of star-strewn skies: all of these things were peripheral in Conway's awareness, as the frame of a picture seen close-up is peripheral in the eye of the viewer. His concentration, to the contrary, was *centered* on the spider, on its eyes.

At the other end of the wire, Lord Daventry waited patiently for an answer. After a little while, wondering at the delay, he asked: "Paul? Are you still there?"

Conway, staring into the vast, crimson, hooded orbs of the thing's eyes where they glared at him hypnotically from the garden, shook his head as if to clear away some mental smog. He finally answered:

"Yes, I'm here. Could you repeat what you said just then? I didn't catch it the first time."

"I said did you see the strange light?"

"No, I saw no light." Conway made no attempt to enlarge upon the subject.

Believing Conway must be tired, the peer decided to keep the conversation short. "Ah…" he cleared his throat. "Look, sorry to be a nuisance, Paul, but I was wondering about old Thomas…" He paused.

Conway made no comment.

"Old Thomas," repeated the peer more loudly, becoming frustrated. "Thomas and his spiders!" His voice came sharp and clear, if a little tinny, from Conway's telephone.

Conway grunted impatiently and frowned. He jiggled the telephone, blew into the ear-piece, and said: "Look, I'm sorry, sir. Terrible line tonight. Can't hear a thing you're saying. Can I ring you back in the morning?" And with that he replaced the receiver.

He was dimly, hazily aware, while he performed these casual, automatic tasks, that the smaller of the two creatures outside bore in its mandibles the body of Andrea Bleaker—that as its mouth worked avidly at her middle, the uppermost of its three globular semi-opaque abdomen-sacks was turning a dull red—but this also was peripheral knowledge. Not once did his attention waver from the eyes of the larger creature. He couldn't divert his attention if he tried.

That night thirty thousand back-up vessels beamed in, an entire task-force, most of them far bigger than the half-dozen or so scout craft already in situ. In the morning Conway made his telephone call, as he had promised, to Lord Daventry, but there was no answer. At midnight a craft had landed in the peer's garden and its pilot had been hungry.

By midday there were still one or two pockets of uninitiated people in isolated places—the odd Eskimo family or settlement, a reclusive order of Tibetan monks, the crew of a marine survey vessel just north of the southern pack ice—all of whom still believed in spiders, but not many. As for the invaders: they were not especially worried about finding these as yet unbranded mavericks. That could wait.

Right now there was the herding to think about, and then the giant factory ships would have to be brought in...

SWAMPED

Now after this, whose gonna be there for any old shrink, eh? Maybe another shrink?

"**S**IR?" MISS POLLACK'S VOICE, enquiring over the intercom. "Are you busy?" She knew I wasn't busy but it sounded good.

"Extremely!" I snapped, doodling in the margin of my newspaper and gloomily considering a crossword clue: *Three across: Exude foraminifers calcareously on the sea floor. Four letters, the third one being a "z," possibly.*

"Sir?" she was impatient.

"Miss Pollack, what is a foraminifer?"

"A rhizopod," She Who Knows Everything (for which reason I employ her, that and the fact that she has pointy tits) answered at once. "Chiefly marine and microscopic."

Rhizopod? The word has a "z" anyway, so there might be a connection at that. "Thank you, Miss Pollack."

"Sir, there's a gentleman to see you," she insisted. "He hasn't an appointment but he says it's urgent—extremely."

We needed the money. "Will you ask him to wait, Miss Pollack, and come in for a moment?"

She came in. "Yes, sir?"

"Does he look like he has money?"

"He looks odd—but then most of them do. I told him your rates and that didn't faze him."

Faze! I glanced quickly at my crossword. Third letter a "z." But no, faze didn't fit. "OK, send him in," I told her; and: "Wait!"

"Sir?"

"What's a rhizopod?"

"A chalk- or chitin-shelled protozoan."

I snapped my fingers. For chalk read calcium! Exude foraminifers *calcareously*!

On her way out, Miss Pollack turned up my air-conditioning, explaining, "He pongs a bit."

"Pardon?"

"He's been *in* something," she wrinkled her nose. "Up to his knees in it!" Then she was through the door and gone.

"Webber," he squeaked moments later, clearing his throat as he squelched into my office and left a trail of green footprints on my neutral-grey carpet. "David Webber."

I stared at him hard and he gazed back for a moment, then turned his face and eyes away. Inferiority complex, possibly. Understandable, since he was so obviously inferior. And from the moment I saw him, and leaped to that conclusion, I knew I was in the wrong line of work. I had suspected it before, but now I knew it.

A psychiatrist must have sympathy for, empathy with, his clients. I didn't even know David-bloody-Webber but already I knew that I could not possibly identify with him and would never, *ever* feel sympathetic toward him. He was…a protozoan, a foraminifer. And, judging by the slime on my carpet, he was aquatic to boot! Amphibian, certainly. I wanted to shout at him, see him cringe, but…we needed the money.

"What can I do for you, Mr. Chitin?—er, Webber?" I asked, standing to glare down on him and crush his hand. He trembled, he sweated; despite the air-conditioning I could smell the *stuff* on his trousers, which looked like he'd been standing in a bowl of very ancient soup for quite a long time.

He shrugged awkwardly. "Not much, I reckon. But—"

"*But?*" I don't like buts.

"But it was your name, Smith, and it was this building."

(God! And I could be doing my crossword puzzle!) "My name is common enough, surely?" I tried to smile encouragingly.

"Not in that place," he said, shuddering. "Nothing is common there! Anyway, it was your *whole* name, Smythe Smith." And he nodded knowingly.

"And this building, you say?" I stood up, led him to my couch, draped one end with pages from the sports section and stretched him out, hands clasped over his abdomen.

"Parallel universe, I think," he told me, blinking rapidly through the thick lenses of his specs. God, he was *ugly*! A real trog!

"Oh, yes?" I nodded understandingly, which they seem to expect of me. "And you've been there, hey?"

"Far too often," he sighed. "Oh, yes indeed!"

I took a pad and pencil, sat down beside him (his top end) and said: "Well you just lie there and decide where to start, and I'll take notes as we go. How does that sound?"

"That's OK," he answered, biting his lip. "Just give me a second, that's all…" His pale brow got all creased up as his thoughts sorted themselves out. And while he was about it, I looked him over closely and tried to discover what it was about him that so irked me.

Possibly it was that he was a nothing. I mean, why bother to be anything at all if you can't be something? Why exist in the first bloody place? Surely not just to foul up my carpet? Lord, how I hated him!

He was, oh, five-foot three inches, about one hundred pounds soaking wet, thirty five years old, pallid, pimply, insect-ravaged, casually clad in a grey cord jacket and trousers, chukka boots and a camouflaged mosquito net neckerchief. And puttees and a pith-helmet! And this was July! Like a poor man's Woody Allen, if that image helps.

I think I hated the pith-helmet worst of all.

Or possibly the fact that he was, unquestionably, very sane. When you've been in the game as long as I have, you know these things instinctively. David Webber was not "a real nut," hardly a "candidate for the funny farm," in no way "a goofball." But yes, he had problems.

"It started," he began, "with the dreams."

"Bad dreams?" (anxiety, possibly.)

"*Very* bad."

"Recurrent dreams?" (Guilt, perhaps?)

"Oh, yes, night after night."

"And always the same dream?" (Obsession!)

"Always."

"—Which you first had when you were a small child?—"

He frowned. "How do you know that?"

"—And which invariably accompanied your...*bedwetting!*"
I was triumphant.

"Bollocks!" he said. "I never wet the bed in my life!"

I was devastated, but: "Go on," I told him, gritting my teeth.

"I was in a swamp," he said, "but a swamp like no swamp
you ever imagined."

"Wait!" I stopped him. "This was a dream?"

"Yes."

"But you mentioned a parallel dimension. Dreams do not
come into that category. Not strictly speaking."

He shrugged. "That's debatable, but—I agree. The parallel
dimension idea didn't come until later—when things started to
follow me back."

"From the swamp, you mean?"

"Yes."

"Like the muck on your trousers, the sports section, my
bloody carpet?" I snapped.

"Well, yes." He shrank down into himself. "Listen, I'm sorry
about—"

"Never shrink!" I told him sternly, cutting him off. "I don't
like the word. And don't ever apologize. It only puts my rates
up. The carpet doesn't matter. I just had it cleaned, that's all. But
do go on."

"That swamp," he said, "is hell! It's alien. There are bugs
with three legs, others with eight. And there are animals with
six legs, but armored like beetles."

"With chitin?" I asked. "Or calcareously?"

He blinked. "What?"

"Like protozoa," I patiently explained. "Tiny little
foraminifers?"

"Hell, no! These are damned *big* things! Some of the bugs
are big as your fist—and they bite! Jesus, you see these bites?"

His face, neck, hands and wrists were quite badly bitten.
"Hence the headgear," I nodded. "And the mosquito net, which

you doubtless drape over the helmet."

"Hey, that's right!" he beamed at me in appreciation, however shyly.

"And the puttees are to keep 'em from getting—"

"—Up my trousers. Right!"

I tried to hide my pleasure. But…maybe he wasn't such a bad guy after all. "Do go on."

"In my dreams I make my way through the swamp. This isn't easy, believe me. As well as the smaller insects and animals there are some real monsters—like prehistoric, you know?"

"Tyrannosaurus," I said.

"At least! And leeches big as squirrels that drop on you out of the creepers! Anyway, I walk toward a place where the tops of buildings are sticking up out of the mud and slime. Now try to get the picture: This is a jungle—a genuine tropical or prehistoric jungle—but not Earth tropics and not Earth prehistory. This is a time-stream which diverged eons ago and went along entirely different lines. It's *another* place, *another* time. A parallel dimension—and weird!"

"So, let's see what we have here. You think your dream is a parallel dimension. You believe that your tiny walnut mind houses an entire world coexistent with this one." (He wasn't mad, I stuck to my guns on that—but *conceited*?)

"Exactly! Coexistent—*and* conterminous!"

"Ah! There's a common boundary. Where, may I enquire? Okefenokee?"

"Here," he said, thumbing himself in the chest.

I rubbed my chin thoughtfully; it's a bore, but another one of those things they seem to expect. "So. *You* are the gateway to and from a parallel world which exists only in your dreams. Is that it?"

"Not quite," he shook his head. "As I've already more than hinted, it exists—and not only in my head!" I backed my chair hastily away from him as, to illustrate his point, something green hopped croaking from the hollow of his neck onto the floor. It was like a tiny frog but it had the wrong number of legs. Croaking again, it hopped under my desk and out of sight.

"*Now no more tricks!*" I shouted, a bit unnerved.

"Man, that's why I'm here!" he shouted back, getting up on his elbows. "You think I can help it? You think I...I *like* it?" He was close to tears.

I pursed my lips, straightened my tie and shrugged (grudgingly.) "The dream—the jungle, the tops of creeper-infested buildings sticking up through the gunge, the leech-squirrels dropping on you, this entire parallel world place which I assure you *doesn't* exist except in your head—just get on with it!"

He lay down again. "You know about entropy?"

"A little. It isn't my problem."

"It's no one's problem, not any more. Entropy isn't. The universe is no longer expanding and expending, it's shrinking, condensing. It's moving back toward another Big Bang. As space shrinks, so does time. Ah, but my argument presupposes that you understand the theory of parallel time-streams."

"I do," I snapped, still smarting from both shrinks, but realizing that the man was simply a peasant, a matter of birth and breeding beyond his control. "At each individual moment of time, every person or thing has an almost infinite choice as to his/her/its course of action, progression. In some far superior time dimension, you did not come in here and I am still happily engaged in pondering the relationship between calcareous mini-crustacea and ocean floor exudations!"

"Correct!" Webber beamed. Then he frowned. "—Except that the choice is now finite. Worse than that, the time-streams are no longer parallel, they are converging. Utterly alien worlds spawned billions of years ago in Earth's nightmare prime—which have evolved along lines as strange as the worlds of distant stars—are now closing in, beginning to impinge upon this one. I am a focal point, a genius loci, a gateway, yes—but I am only *one* gateway. There may well be others!"

"Explanation time," I told him. "You are obsessed with your dream, your daydream, your delusion. But it *is* a delusion, believe me. You are not mad, not yet, but you are sickening—" (he really *was* sickening!) "—which is why I now suggest a course of treatment and, ultimately, a cure."

"God, only let it be so!" he breathed a sigh of relief. "I

mean, sooner or later it's going to get me. On my way here, in broad daylight, in the middle of a city street, for Christ's sake, suddenly I was there, up to my knees in it! See?" he pointed at his slimy trousers. "I was only there for a second, then back on the street again, but—"

"But me no buts!" I said, holding up my hands and turning my face away. "Have I not explained? You are deluded, a victim of your mind's fictions."

"This slime is real," he said.

"But it does *not* issue from a swamp in some alien, parallel world!"

"Where then? You think I carry buckets of the stuff around with me? And when the mood is on me I simply pour it over my trousers? Is that what you're saying?"

"No, no—" (I thought hard) "—it is, perhaps, a poltergeist phenomenon. You do it to yourself. Psychosomatic self-persecution. ESP. Parapsychology."

"And—" (something slithered slimily away from his crotch, plopped onto the floor and shot under the desk to do battle with the frog-thing) "—What, may I ask, of these things?"

"Ectoplasm!" I answered. "And extremely icky ectoplasm at that. Involuntary psychic, er, exudations, yes! You would appear to house—" I considered it, "—not a parallel dimension, but a gungergeist!"

"Eh?"

"A word of my own manufacture," I shrugged it off expansively. "A slime-slinging ghost."

"Rid me of it!" he cried. "Exorcise the bloody thing!"

"I will, I will," I placated him. "But first tell me more about the dream. I hate to admit it—but it's interesting."

He composed himself. "Where was I? Oh, yes: So I get to this building—or rather the top of this building—and there's an old, rotting flagpole, bending over with its burden of creepers and what have you, and there's a tatty rag of a flag flying away up there above the groping, slimy green foliage. I run it down and read what it says. It's moldy, of course—everything in that place is moldy—but I can still make out what it says."

"Yes?"

"It says 'Möebler Enterprises.'"

"Ah!"

"It's *this* building, do you see?"

"Certainly this is the Möebler Building," I answered. "Indeed it is—and I am required to pay inordinate fees for the use of these offices in said edifice—which is to say my time is limited and I allocate only so much to each client. Please go on, and hurry! You are on top of the Möebler Building, which protrudes from the surface of a mighty swamp. What happens then?"

"That's where you come in, he said. "And that's why I'm here. It was too much of a coincidence. See, after I've read what's on the flag, I look around and there's this piece of wood, eighteen inches by six, chamfered edges, black paint flaking off, gold lettering still intact, floating on the quag—and the gold letters spell your name! "Smythe Smith: Psychiatrist.'"

"Hmm!" (Hmms are useful, if only to fill gaps.) "So it seems your fantasy has suggested its own cure—or rather, it has signposted the way to that salvation."

"Perhaps," he seemed wary, "But on the other hand, it could be a warning."

"Explain."

"Well, in order to reach this bit of wood, this name-plate—which, incidentally, is that selfsame plank which adorns the door entering into these rooms, and which I noted upon entering is loose and about to detach itself—I reach out, and inadvertently step off the parapet of the building: The roof, that is, which lies, as does the entire city, under the slop. And down I go in the filth, which tugs at me like quicksand. I grab a creeper and it snaps, sink up to my knees. But then my feet strike a ledge, I stop sinking, and—"

"You wake up!"

"Yes, thank God!" He shuddered pitifully and I found myself wishing I could pity him.

"My solution is expensive," I told him then.

"So what's money?"

"Even more expensive," I told him. "I propose to hypnotize you, revisit your dream, then neatly excise it—or exorcise it, if you insist—utterly from your conscious and unconscious minds, so that it may never return. My instrument of excision shall be a simple post-hypnotic command."

"You're going to put me to sleep?" He seemed alarmed, and for the first time I noticed the sagging dark bags under his eyes.

"You certainly look like you could use it!" I said.

"But I can't sleep, I mustn't, I daren't! Can't you see that?"

I sighed. "But that is precisely why you must! Don't you bloody listen to anything anyone tells you?"

"Knowing I have to be rid of it doesn't make me any less frightened of it," he said, logically. "It's like a vast version of a bad tooth! An entire mouthful of them!"

"Then you accept my proposition?"

"Only if you'll guarantee it will work."

"I guarantee you'll be no worse off."

"Very well…"

"So lie back and relax. Good. Close your eyes. Think sleep. God how you need sleep. You are really *knackered*! Man, you're shagged out! You're going to go to sleep right now, you're so tired. Even my words are losing their meaning. Everything is losing its meaning. What the hell is meaning? There *is* no meaning, only sleep, sleep, sleep. When I say to you 'calcareous foraminifers' you will fall instantly into a deep, deep, deep, deep sleep. Here we go: 'Calcareous foraminifers!'"

He snored.

"Where are you?"

"Möebler Building," he mumbled.

"On top of it?"

"Inside it. Private consultation room of—"

"Yes, I know that!" I snapped. "But what are you doing there?"

"Sleeping."

"Good! Now, do you remember the swamp?"

"God, yes!"

"I want you to go there. Go there now."

He began to move fitfully, cursed under his breath, twitched and grimaced.

"Are you there?"

"Yes."

"OK. Now then, keeping an eye peeled for squirrel-leeches, make your way to the place with the flagpole. Yes, that's it, over there. Fight your way through the swamp toward it. Careful, you nearly trod on a plesiosaur just then! But now you can see the place in the murky distance, the tatty flag fluttering over the misty green canopy of—"

"Can it!" he mumbled. "I'm there already."

"Don't anticipate me!" I snarled. "OK, so you've read the flag and you know that this is the Möebler Building. Now you see the name-plate which you try to reach, and—"

"*Shit*! he yelped, floundering there on my couch.

"The slime is covering your shoulders, your neck, lapping at your chin."

"Get me out of—*glug*!" His mouth gaped and his chest heaved. He gulped desperately for air but that didn't seem to work.

I grabbed at his suddenly flailing arms, trapped his hands, began to draw him upright. "It's OK, I can save you. See, I can pull you free from the slime. I can save you from your dream, your obsession, your fantasy. I can—"

What the hell? He weighed half a ton—literally! This little shrivelled guy—and me, built like a brick conservatory. And he was slipping from my grip, squeezing back down onto the couch, sucked down by the slop. This was one tough bastard gungergeist, all right!

"When I snap my fingers and say 'rhizopod exudations,'" I changed my tack, "all of this—this entire fantasy and all that's causing it—will disappear utterly, forever, and you will wake up. Do you understand?"

"*Glug-glug-glug*!"

"And you will never, never, *ever* dream that dream or imagine that fantasy or suffer that aberration again, right?"

"*Glug-glug*! *Argh*! *Glug-arrgghhh*!" He stopped flopping about, lay still, head lolling. It stopped lolling. His eyes popped open. They glazed over.

"David Webber," I snapped my fingers, "'rhizopod exudations!'"

He was as dead as a doornail. So? The way I see it, he was no worse off. But—

Damn! Never let a client die on you before you collect. It is the first tenet of good medicine, be it of mind or body.

I heard Miss Pollack scream from next door, rushed in to see what had upset her. I was in time to see the other door slam shut as she left, still screaming, and to hear my loose wooden name-plate clatter to the tiles out in the corridor. Then I saw what had frightened here: an electric-blue Pteranodon perched in the open window, scratching its long beak on a filing cabinet. I waved my arms at it and the thing flapped away.

Then I hurried back to Webber, and saw that I had failed doubly. No, not that, never *that!* But I saw, in fact, that he had been right. There had been no cure for him. The battle had been uneven; I had been beaten before I began. Quite simply: Reversed entropy is incurable.

For Webber *was* a gateway, one of many, I suspect, and something was even now coming through.

Consider: In this dimension he was so much dead meat, an inert mass, whose internal and external pressures matched precisely. But in that other place he was an empty bag sinking in a primal goo which was determined to fill him as its external pressure increased with the rate and depth of his descent.

And out from his open mouth the stuff began to slop, then belch, then gush: a flood I knew could never be staunched. Or at least, not until it was as deep as this bloody building!

The time-streams were converging. Things were already floundering about in the mire and one of them even made a bad-tempered assault on my right foot! I kicked it away, snatched up my paper and backed out of the room, out of the office.

Not waiting for the elevator I ran down ten flights of stairs and out onto the street, there pausing to straighten my tie. A block away, to the east, at the corner of the next junction, something like a quinceratops munched automobiles in the middle of the road. In any case, that wasn't my route. Turning to walk the other way, I heard glass shatter and looked up. Others craned their necks, *oohing* and *aahing*.

Ten stories up my office window had shattered outwards,

raining glass and goo into the street. Droplets of slime splashed on my face like thick rain. Now the building was spewing great gobs of the stuff, which oozed lumpily down the walls like—

Oozed?

Great leaping protozoa—*ooze!*

Exude foraminifers calcareously on the sea floor.

I paused to lean against the wall, take out my pen and fill in the crossword—but only for a moment. Beneath my feet, trapped under a sewer grating, something belched and blustered.

Then—

There was much to do. Fortunately, as well as my apartment in the city, I owned a hunting shack up in the mountains. And anyway, I was long overdue for a vacation.

Joining the suddenly fleeing throng. I ran west. (Actually, with the Big Bang still four and a half billion years away, there seemed little point in hurrying.)

But I ran, anyway...

A REALLY GAME BOY

And I ask you, what's in a single word, eh?

Yes, you're right, Sheriff, Willy Jay *is* a real game boy, and I counts myself lucky he's my friend. And I really do 'preciate the point that he ain't been home for more'n a week, (a whole week! Dun't that beat all?) but iffen we was to stop him now—why, he'd never fergive us!

As to the folks sayin' *I* got somethin' to do with him bein' missin'—why, I really dun't believe that. Everyone knows how much I love that boy! He's the onliest kid 'round here has anythin' to do with me. Hell, most o' the kids is even a mite scared o' me! Well, they shouldn't do the things they do and then I wouldn't git mad.

And you know as well as I do how many heads Willy's rattled 'cause he heard them a-callin' me. *That's* how close Willy Jay and me is, Sheriff, and you can believe it. And that's why I cain't tell you where he's at.

Now listen, Sheriff, you dun't scare me none. My Paw says that iffen I dun't want to talk to you I sure dun't have to, and that dang him but it might be best iffen I dun't say nothin' anyhow. And anyways, Willy made me promise.

See, it's a kind o' endurance test—that's what Willy called it, a endurance test—and he wouldn't thank me none for lettin' you break it up. Not now he's gone this long. Sure is a game boy, that Willy …

Tell you all about it?

Well, I s'pose I could. I mean, that's not like tellin' you where he's at. See, I cain't do that. 'Cause iffen you stopped him he'd surely blame me, and I values his friendship too much to lose it just 'cause I shot my mouth off to the town Sheriff. I mean, Sheriff—what did you ever do for me, eh?

Hey, I knows you laugh at me behind my back. Paw told me you do. He says that you're the two-facedest Sheriff he ever knowed.

What's that you say? Well what's that got to do with it, Willy bein' just thirteen and me eighteen and all? He's a real big kid for thirteen, and he treats me just like a brother. Why, I could tell you secrets me and Willy knows that would—

—But I wun't ...

There you go again, blamin' me for that little Emmy-May kid what drowned. You think I did that? Why, it was me drug her out the water! And Willy with me. It was a accident she fell in the crick, that's all, and I never did take her clothes offen her like some tried to say I did. That was just Willy foolin' about with her. He didn't mean her no real harm, but—

Aw, see? I promised him I'd never say a word 'bout that, and there you go trickin' me into shootin' off my mouth again. Well, okay, I'll tell you—but you got to promise me you'll never tell Willy.

Okay...

It was like this:

See, Willy took a shine to that little Emmy-May girl and he wanted to sort of kiss her and do things! Aw, shucks, Sheriff, you *knows* what sort o' things! Anyways, she bein' a Sunday school girl and all, he figures maybe she ain't much for that kind o' thing. So bein' a game boy and all, and not lettin' nothin' stop him once he's set hissen mind on somethin', Willy works out a little trick to play on her. So this Sunday Willy gets re-ligion and off he goes to Sunday school. When it's over and all the kids is a-leavin', he catches up to Emmy-May and asks her iffen he can see her home. See, she's seen him hangin' back, and she's sort o' hung back too, so maybe she's taken a shine to him like he has to her.

Anyways, their walkin' takes 'em close to Fletcher's Spinney where the crick bends, and this was part o' Willy's plan. I was a-waitin' in the spinney, all crouchin' down and out o' sight like he told me to be, and I seen and heard it all.

"I knows a secret place," says Willy, his face all eyes and teeth and smiles.

"Oh?" says Emmy-May, and she laughs. "You're just foolin' about, Willy Jay," she tells him. "Why, there ain't no secret places 'round here!"

"Is so," he says. "C'mon and I'll show you—but you got to keep it a secret."

"Sure thing!" she says, all big-eyed, and they runs into the spinney.

Anyways, sure 'nough there is a secret place: a clearin' where the grass is kind o' cropped under a big old oak that leans right out over the crick. Me and Willy had fixed up a rope there and used to swing right out over the crick and back. And sometimes we'd take our clothes off and splash down into the water off the rope. O' course, me and Willy can swim like we was born to the water …

So there they are in the secret place, and me creepin' close in the shrubs and listenin' and a-watchin' it all.

"See," says Willy, "this here's my secret place. And that's my swing. Why, I can swing right over the crick on that there rope!"

"Can you really, Willy?" says Emmy-May.

"Sure 'nough. Watch!" says he. And he takes a run at the rope, grabs it and swings right over the crick and back. "Iffen I'd let go I could've landed on the other side," he says. "Would you like to try the swing, Emmy-May?"

"Oh, no!" she holds back. "I cain't swim, and iffen I fell—"

Willy, he nods and lets it be. "Anyways," says he, "it's just a pre-caution, is all."

"A what? What sort of precaution, Willy?" she asks.

"Why, the rope!" says he. "In case I got to run."

"From what?" she laughs. "Ain't nothin' here'bouts to be a-feared of."

"Oh?" says he. "What about wood spirits, eh? Surely you knows about them? My Paw says your Maw and Paw is full o' superstition from the old country."

"Oh, I *knows* about them," she answers, "but like you say, them's just old wives' tales." But still she looks around the clearin' real careful like.

By now they's a-sittin' under the old oak and this is where I'm to play my part in this joke. See, Sheriff, Willy had it all figured out. I just rustled a bush a little and let out a low sort o' groan, like a hant might make.

"What was that?" asks Emmy-May, and she creeps real close to Willy and puts her arms around his neck.

"Did you hear 'im?" says Willy, actin' all s'prised. "Ordinary folk dun't hear 'im, mostly."

"Hear who?" she whispers, her blue eyes big and round.

"That mean old wood spirit," says Willy. "But dun't you worry none. Oh, he's ugly and he's mean, but iffen you're a good friend o' mine he wun't hurt you. He's only ever real bad on full moon nights."

She hugs his neck tighter. "Tonight's a full moon, Willy Jay," she whispers.

"Is it?" again he looks s'prised. "Why, so it is! But that's okay. Just be still and quiet. As long as you're with me he wun't hurt you. We gets along just fine, me and the wood spirit—mostly." And he gives her a kiss full on her mouth.

Now she pulls back from him and stands up—just like he'd told me she might. I rustles the bush some more and makes a angry sort of grunt, and Willy says, "I *told* you to stay still, Emmy-May! Dun't you know them wood spirits is dangerous? Now come back down here."

So she gets down again, all shivery like, and Willy pulls the bow at her neck and loosens her buttons. Well, Sheriff, by now I'm all excited. I mean me?—I'd never *ever* dare do any sech a thing, but dang me iffen Willy ain't the gamest boy. But ... that Emmy-May is sort o' game, too. She slaps him real hard. And me, watchin', I sees his face go all red from the slap.

"So," he says, breathin' real hard. "That's how it's a-goin' to be, is it? Well, I warned you, Emmy-May." And he calls out: "Wood spirit, you see this here girl, Emmy-May?" I gives a big grunt and shakes my bush. "Well, she dun't like me and she dun't believe in you. There," he says to her. "Serves you right, Emmy-May, for slappin' me. Your folks'll sure miss you tonight!"

That was my signal to make some real angry growlin' and snarlin', and to beat on the ground with a fallen branch. And I set the bushes a-shakin' like they was full of rattlers as I crept closer, pantin' like a wild animal.

"Call 'im off, Willy Jay!" Emmy-May cries. She hugs Willy tight and sobs, and this time when he kisses her she dun't protest none. And when he puts his hand up her dress she sobs a little but she dun't stop him none. Then he stands up, real slow like, and takes off his clothes, every last stitch. And his pecker is big as my own, Sheriff, I swear it. He's a real big boy for thirteen …

"What you a-doing', Willy Jay?" she says, all breathless like.

"Wood spirit," he calls out. "Iffen she's good to me you just stay quite—but iffen she ain't …"

Emmy-May starts in a-sobbin' real loud.

"And iffen she dun't stop her snivellin' right this minute—then she's all your'n!"

"Willy! Willy!" she cries, crawlin' to his feet.

"Take off your clothes," he says, his voice all broke up like. "All of 'em, and do it slow."

"But Willy," she gasps, "I—"

"Wood spirit!" he calls, and I gives a real loud howl, so like a wolf it scares even me!

So she takes her clothes off and stands there all pink and sweet and shivery and a-tryin' to cover herself up with her hands, and even the hot summer sun comin' through the oak's branches cain't warm her none. And Willy, he lies her down in the grass and touches, pokes, strokes and kisses her here and there and everywhere, and—

Well, I'm *a-comin'* to that, Sheriff!

Finally, he's all worked up and his face is red and his hands a-shakin'. He says: "Open your legs real wide, Emmy-May, so's I can put my pecker in you."

"I'll tell, I'll tell!" she screams, and she jumps up.

Quick as a flash Willy yells: "Sic 'er, wood spirit—sic 'er good!" But she ain't listenin' none.

That was when the accident happened. See, she made a run at the rope, jumped, fell—

Well, I sprung up out o' hidin' and was all fixed to dive right in after her, but Willy grabs me and says: "Dun't fret yourself, Zeb," he says. "She swims real good…" Only he was mistook, 'cause she couldn't. And the crick bein' pretty fast water just there and all…

Down she went and swept away, and her head bobbin' in the current as she's whirled out of sight. Willy, he tosses her clothes in after her and gets hisself dressed real quick. "C'mon, Zeb," he says, "and I'll tell you what we'll do. We'll say we was walkin' by the crick and we saw her in the water. Mind, we dun't know as to how she got there."

Then we races near a mile to the big swimmin' hole where the kids is all splashin' and a-yellin'. And Willy shouts, "There's a girl in the water, comin' down the crick! We seen her!" And as Emmy-May comes driftin' into view we both go in full-dressed and drag her out. But by then she's a goner.

So you see, Sheriff, it were a accident. Just Willy's little trick gone a mite wrong, is all.

Now I done *told* you he ain't run away! What, because o' what happened to Emmy-May, you mean? Shucks, why that weren't nothin' compared to the other things. I mean, it were a accident. But then there was your prize hens, and—

Oh. My! I didn't *ever* mean to mention them hens, Sheriff, I surely did not. Well, you shouldn't whacked his ear that time he gave Jason Harbury a bloody nose. That really made him sore, Sheriff. Oh, it were Willy, all right. He pizzened 'em good! And then there's Old Miss Littlewood …

Why sure, Sheriff, I knows she's dead.

Well, see, Willy had this thing he'd do with worms. It tickled me pink and made the girls all throw up, and Willy—heh! heh!—such a *game* boy, that one!

See, he'd find a big, juicy worm and pop it in his mouth, then let it just sort o' dribble out, all wrigglin', when someone'd stop to speak to him—'specially girls.

One day he'd trapped Old Miss Littlewood's cat and tied a can to his tail, then let him loose over the old lady's fence. Why, that cat was madder'n all hell! Finally she grabbed him and got the can off of him, and she came over to the fence where we was hidin' in the bushes.

She sees us and says: "Zeb, I just knows you wouldn't do a thing like that. But you, Willy Jay—'bout you I ain't so sure. You are one mean, cruel, unpleasant boy, Willy—and you'll end up in a sorry mess sure as shootin'!"

And Willy, he just stands up all slow like, and he opens his mouth and grins, and a big fat worm glides over his bottom lip and falls plop onto the grass!

Well, she screams! She really screams!—and Willy just standin' there laughin'. Until she reaches across that fence and brings him such a smack as I never heard. That did it. Willy bein' such a game boy and all, he wa'n't a-goin' to let no old spinster lady get away with that! No sir!

We spent the next hour or two diggin' out the biggest, fattest, juiciest worms we could find, and when Old Miss Littlewood left her house and walked off down the street and into town with her basket, then that Willy he snuck into the house and put worms in her bed, and her kitchen, in her preserves, her butter, her milk … worms everywhere!

T'ward dusk she comes home, goes in, lights her lamp, and for a while we can hear her a-hummin' through the open window. Then—she starts a-screamin'. And she keeps right on a-screamin', each scream higher'n the last. Woke all the neighbours, and all their lights goin' on, and me and Willy watchin' the house and a-sniggerin' fit to bust. Then she comes staggerin' out in her nightdress, trips and falls in the garden—and lies still. Me and Willy, we gits out o' there fast!

Yes, I know folks said she'd had a stroke or heart attack or suthin', and so she did. But what *caused* it, eh?

Now, Sheriff, I allow I didn't much care for that one. I mean, when I saw Willy the next day and he laughed at her bein' dead and all. But when he saw I wa'n't too happy 'bout it he soon dried up and said yes, I was right. But it had been a accident, just like Emmy-May, and iffen folks found out I'd be in real trouble 'cause I helped him dig them worms. But, him bein' my friend and all, he said not to worry my head none—he wouldn't tell on me. I was just to fergit the whole thing…

Now Sheriff, I done told you already I cain't—

What?

Just tell you what the endurance test is all about? Well, I suppose that'd be okay. So long as you dun't ask me where it's at.

See, Willy has this thing 'bout ropes and climbin' and
a-swingin'—a reg'lar Tarzan, he is. Well, one day we was at—
the place. No, sir, not the secret place in Fletcher's Spinney, the
place o' the endurance test. And there's this rope a-hangin', see.
And Willy says, "Hey, Zeb, you're pretty big and strong. Iffen
that rope was round your feet, how long you reckon you could
hang up there, all upside down like, afore you had to stop?"

"Why, I really cain't say as I knows that, Willy Jay," says I.

"I reckon," says he, "I could beat your time whatever."

"Now Willy," says I, "you're a real game boy and no
question, but I beat you at runnin', swimmin', wrestlin' and
swingin'—so what makes you think you could outlast me on
that there rope?"

Willy, I dun't think he liked bein' reminded I could beat him
at them things. He got that stubborn look on his face and said:
"But I could beat you this time, Zeb, I knows I could."

"Willy, you're a real winner," says I, "and my onliest true
friend, too—but I'm older, bigger and stronger'n you. Now you
think real clever and no question, but you're just thirteen and—"

"I can beat you!" he says.

"Okay," says I. "I believe it."

"No," says he, "that ain't no proof. This here's a endurance
test, Zeb, and we got to try it out."

"Now, Willy," says I, "I got a good many chores to do for
Paw. Iffen I'm not home an hour from now, he'll—"

"You first," says Willy.

See, it makes no matter no how arguin' with him when
he's in that there stubborn mood o' hissen. So we climbs up
and hauls up the rope and he ties it round my feet in a noose.
Then I climbs back down and lets go and swings to and fro 'til
I'm all still, and Willy Jay sits up there lookin' down at me and
a-grinnin'. "There you go," says he, and he keeps the time.

Now then, Sheriff, after 'bout an hour or so Willy says, "Hey,
Zeb! You all right down there?"

"Sure," says I. "My ears is a mite poundin', and I got pins
and needles in my legs—but I'm okay, Willy Jay."

"Sure?"

"Sure, I'm sure!"

"Well, enough is enough," he says, soundin' a bit sore at me. I can't say why he's sore, but he sounds it. "You better come on up now, 'cause it's time you was a-startin' home to them chores o' your'n"

"But what about the endurance test?" says I.

"Well, we'll finish it another day," he says.

So I clumb up—but truth to tell I nearly didn't make it, my arms and legs was so stiff and all. And I got the rope off and staggered about and stamped my feet 'til I could feel 'em again. "How long'd I do?" I asks.

"Oh, an hour and three and a half minutes," says Willy, sort of half-sneerin' like.

"Hey!" says I. "I could go a lot longer but for them chores. Why, I could go another ten or twenty minutes easy!"

"Oh, sure!" says he. "Listen," he says, "I beat you hands down, Zeb. I could stay up that there rope a whole week iffen I wanted to ..."

Now that was boastin' pure and simple and I knowed it.

"Willy," says I, "ain't nobody—but nobody—could do that! Why, you'd git all hungry, and how'd you sleep?"

"Hell!" he says. "There's meat enough on my bones, Zeb. I'd not crave feedin'. And as for sleepin'—well, bats do it, dun't they? They spends all winter a-hangin' and a-sleepin'. Hell, I bet I could do that too, iffen I put my mind to it."

"Well all I knows," says I, "is that I'm real glad I'm down after only one hour, three and a half minutes, that's all."

"You're you and I'm me, Zeb," he says, "but I can see you needs convincin'. Okay, how long's them chores o' your'n a-goin' to take?"

"Oh, 'bout an hour, I reckon."

"Okay," says he. "I'm a-goin' to tie up my feet right now and hang here 'til you gets back." And he did. And hangin' there, he says: "Now this is stric'ly 'tween you and me, our secret. Dun't you dare tell a soul 'bout this, hear? See, I'm a-goin' to stick my thumbs in my belt, like this—" and he did, "—and just rest here easy like. And I'm a-goin' to concentrate. Now dun't you go breakin' my concentration nohow, Zeb, hear?"

And I said, "Okay."

"Iffen I feels like hangin' here a week, you just let me hang, right?"

"Right," says I. But o' course, I dun't believe he can do it.

"So off you go and do your chores, Zeb Whitley, and I'll be right here when you gits back."

"Okay," I says again, and I scoots.

Well, I was late home and Paw gives me some talkin' to. Then I did my chores—chopped firewood, fetched-n'-carried, this and that—until I figured I was all through. A good hour was up by then, but Paw saw me a-headin' off and says: "Hey, boy! Where you a-goin'?"

"Why, nowheres, Paw."

"Danged right!" says he. "You was late, and so you can do some more chores. I got a whole list for you." And he kept me right at it all evenin' 'til dark come in. After that—well, I ain't allowed out after dark, Sheriff. Paw says he dun't want no trouble, and people bein' ready to lay the blame too quick and all, it's best he knows where I'm at after dark. So off I goes to bed.

But when I hears him a-snorin', up I jumps and runs to … to the place o' the endurance test. And wouldn't you know it? There he is a-hangin' in the dark, quiet as a bat, all concentratin', his thumbs tucked in his belt just like afore. And Lord, he's been there all of five or six hours! And him so quiet, I figures maybe he's a-sleepin' just like he said he could. So I just tippy-toed out o' there and snuck home and back to bed.

Anyhow, next mornin' Paw gets a note from Uncle Zach over the hill, sayin' please come and bring big Zeb, 'cause Uncle Zach's a-clearin' a field and there's work a-plenty. And hey!—that was excitin'! I mean, I really do like Uncle Zach and him me. So Paw hitches up the wagon and off we goes, and we're all the way to Uncle Zach's place afore I remembers Willy.

By now he'll be down off of that rope for sure and madder'n all hell, I reckon, 'cause I wa'n't there to check his time. But heck!—he beat me every which ways anyhow…

And we was at Uncle Zach's six days.

This mornin' we comes home, and soon's Paw's done with me I gits on over to … to the place o' the endurance test, and—

That's right, Sheriff! Now how'd you guess that? Sure 'nough, he's still up there. Nearly a week, and that spunky boy still a-hangin' by his feet. So I goes up to him—but not too close, 'cause it's all shut in and hot and all, and the summer flies is bad and the place stinks some—and I says: "Willy, you been here six days and seven nights and some hours, and you sure beat the hell out o' me! You see that old clock out there over the schoolhouse? It's near noon o' the seventh day. Dun't you reckon you should come on down now, Willy Jay?" And I reaches up and gives him a little prod.

Sheriff, are you okay? You sure do look groggy, Sheriff...

Well, I shouldn't prodded Willy like that 'cause I guess it spoils his concentration. Down comes a arm real slow and creaky like, and it points to the door. He's a tellin' me to git out, he ain't finished yet! So off I goes, and I'm a-comin' up the street when you grabs me and—

Why, yes, I did say I could see the schoolhouse clock from the place o' the endur—

Aw, Sheriff! You're just too danged clever for your own good. You guessed it. That's right, Old Man Potter's livery—and him away visitin' and all. His old barn, sure—but dun't you go disturbin' Willy none, or—

Okay, okay, I'm a-comin'—but I just knows there'll be trouble. He told me not to say a word, and there I goes blabbin' and a-blabbin'. And he wun't thank me none for bringin' you down on him, Sheriff, and that's a fact. Okay, I'll be quiet ...

Oh, sure, I knows the door's shut and bolted, Sheriff, but there's a loose board there, see? Yes, sir, you're right, it is a danged hot summer. And did you ever see so many flies? Only quiet now, or you'll disturb Willy.

See him there? Yes sir, Sheriff, I knows it's gloomy, but—

Hey! Lookit them flies go when you touched him! And ... Sheriff? Are you sure you're feelin' okay, Sheriff?

What?

The rope was too tight 'round his ankles? His blood pooled and swelled up his belly? His belt got wedged under his ribs, you say, and trapped his thumbs? And he's ... he's...

No! You must be mistook, Sheriff Tuttle. Just give him

another little shake and you'll see how wrong you are. Why, he'll go up that rope like a monkey up a stick, all a laughin' and—

But he *cain't* be dead, not Willy! He's just a-concentratin', that's all. Maybe he's a-sleepin' even, like them bats do. What, Willy Jay—dead?

See! See! I'm right. I done *told* you, Sheriff. See what he's a-doin' now? That there's his worm trick!

Dang me, Willy Jay, but I never seen you get *that* many in your mouth afore—you really *game* boy!

A DREAMER'S TALE

But you've been warned about that, right?

Myself? Well, I've always been something of a dreamer; as a child, as a youngster in my teens, and even now, as a middling old man. For what is a person without his aspirations, his hopes, his dreams? As for the first of these—my *waking* desires and ambitions—they haven't worked out as I hoped, not entirely. But do they ever, I mean for anyone? There are so many people I've met or heard of who have aspired (to what hardly matters; a diversity of things, be it riches, celebrity, or even notoriety) and among them some who actually fulfilled their desires, even if they didn't seem to know it. For never *really* satisfied, they continued to lust after what-ever it was that always seemed to retreat to a place beyond their reach. The expert mountaineer and his thoughts of the next highest unclimbed peak, which might even kill him—but ah, the glory! The billionaire, who dreams of the Bank or England, and perhaps even the keys which will give him unrestricted access to Fort Knox—and so much more money than he can actually spend, even if he wanted to! The champion swimmer with many medals and a home with an Olympic-sized pool—yet plans to build another palatial dwelling in the South of France, right there on the rim of the Mediterranean! (And how's *that* for a pool? But hey, what about the South Pacific?)

Do you see what I mean?

So much for them, then. But *my* hopes and ambitions have scarcely seemed to materialize at all, and perhaps that's why I've felt it necessary to dwell so much more and travel so widely in dreams…if not yet to that ultimate, unknown destination where I might finally say, "And now at last I've had it all! There *is* nothing else beyond this place, this fantastic terminus." Which for me could be where my every last aspiration reaches its climax and expires—

—But not yet, and not I fear for quite a while yet, if ever…

But then again, dreams are only dreams…aren't they? Well, maybe so, but on occasion I've read about, or met up with and talked to, people who believe that the subconscious world is so much more than that; met them in my dreams, of course. People like Randolph Carter, whom I came across when visiting Ulthar, where no man may kill a cat, nor even dare imagine so evil a deed! And Kuranes, another ex-waking worlder—now the Lord of Ooth-Nargi, Celephais, and the Sky around Serranian—in his manor-house on the ever wild and dramatic Cornish-seeming coast. Or David Hero and Eldin the Wanderer, those rough-diamond adventurers who, despite being permanent dreamers now, still haven't achieved their ultimate Earth-born ambitions…or might they just possibly be of that extremely rare species which has and in fact is achieving it, without even realizing that the predestined and inevitable is already upon them?

But as I have discovered, the aspirations of men and the lands and worlds they dream are as varied as the dreams themselves, a great many of which should never have been dreamed in the first place; the most mutable and hideous of which may so swiftly and terrifyingly turn into nightmares!

Which brings me to my own latest dream, a strange one that never for a moment anticipated the Elysium I was seeking, not even from its enigmatic beginning. And yet, paradoxically…

But first let me let me tell you about it, and then you can decide for yourself…

It was in the mid-afternoon of a gloomy yet oppressively warm and vaporous day that I climbed a rough, seemingly forgotten and definitely uncared for road of frequently zigzagging fissures where coarse, bulging weeds and thrusting brambles had long-since displaced and even upended the moss-grown cobbles. Ascending on aching feet toward the lower crest of a long rise or ridge of barrier hills, and weary from my efforts as I reached the central summit, I began to observe a town where it expanded however gradually into view at the edge of what appeared to be a perfectly ordinary ocean of grey wavelets, foaming on a shingle shore. Indeed, I had spent my waking life in a reasonably similar town...or so I thought. Until, as I began to make my way down the badly dilapidated and in places crumbling surface of the once-road's nevertheless welcome descent, the actual differences slowly became rather more apparent.

The town was at the hub of three roads, one of which was the downhill course I was pursuing while the others ran parallel to the coastline, one entering from the north and blending with the suburbs, the other from the south; though how I arrived at or became aware of this orientation I can't say, except to explain that in my dreams knowledge of certain peripheral matters seems to be instinctive; the same for most of us dreamers, I imagine.

However, and apart from the question of directions, the condition of the coast roads seemed consistently poor, even as the degraded road which I so carefully negotiated. I could have been mistaken, of course; the town's outermost structures— the tall gates of its encircling wall and the lesser lanes and suburban buildings within—were still at least a mile and a half away, and the coast roads somewhat farther yet, and yet more indistinct. Moreover, and while there appeared to be activity of sorts in the town (however cautious-seeming and performed often as not by people in small swiftly moving groups,) there was little or nothing of mechanized vehicular motion, but only that of horse-drawn drays or small hand carts on the apparently abandoned roads.

Also, the entire scene was overcast by a warm, wispy grey cloud cover, and to make matters worse it appeared that in my dreams my eyesight had suffered with age even as when awake! No, I am not blind—not yet, not at all—but things often seem very dim and vague, (very dreamy?) and ridiculous personal vanity doesn't permit of spectacles; more especially in my dreams, where I like to pretend I'm much younger...

But let me not stray too far from my story, which I'm sure can be scarcely different from certain of your own subconscious imaginings, though as I proceed you might begin to wish it was—and in particular the very darkest of your fantasies...

Halfway down the slope toward the town, my route was paralleled by a meandering stream that eventually passed beneath me where it wandered under the single arch of a sturdy stone bridge. Beneath the bridge the stream had filled something of a hollow, deepening and broadening into a pool before resuming its vagrant course...to wherever? To the town itself, I supposed. A group of male children, mainly pre-teenagers, were playing in the pool, racing each other crosswise to and fro in a variety of swimming styles. They were strangely quiet, so it was not until I was almost directly overhead that I heard their splashing and curiously subdued chatter. Then, leaning against the chest-high wall of the bridge to gaze down on these young lads where they played no more than nine or ten feet below me, I called out:

"Hello there, boys! A good day for a cooling swim, most definitely. But...is there no school today?"

Before the words were out of my mouth entirely, the splashing and quiet mutterings had died away, leaving the group to crane their necks, staring up at me wide-eyed from where they now stood stock still and utterly silent in the shallow reaches of the water...until the oldest and biggest of them replied: "School, Sir? What school? There's only school in the mornings, and then only on the brightest days. Days when the shadows stand out sharp and clear, and there's naught to fear in them...or more especially to fear in those *without* them! But wait right there, if you don't mind, Sir, so that I may check?" With which he left me wondering about the meaning of his strange comments as he got out of the pool, climbed its bank up, around and onto the road, and approached me—but not too closely and plainly ready to run—with many a start whenever I moved however calmly; as when I took out my pipe and long matches, and sucked a flame into momentary being in the bowl of dark, compacted baccy.

Standing there barefooted in dripping short trousers, he studied me head to toe—especially my feet and the cobbles around—openly if nervously, and I thought to hear a sigh of relief as he nodded his apparent approval and said, "Your shadow is sharp, Sir, even without the sun. And I'm sorry if we seem rude, but always best to be careful—even in broad daylight."

"Oh, I'm sure it is!" I told him, thinking, *Maybe he's not in full possession of his faculties, poor lad!* By which time he had got up onto the wall and jumped down again into the deepest part of the pool. "And I couldn't help noticing," I called down to him, where he stood as before staring up at me, "that you have a pretty sharp shadow yourself!" Which might have made little sense, but showed that I was at least willing to take part in his game or fantasy, whatever.

"At night too," he called back, "in the lamplight. And that's a most important thing—and one of the most frightening—the way they shorten and lengthen uncertainly as we move beneath the flaring light…!"

The younger kids were all chattering again, but once more quietly as I shook my head before continuing on my way. And by then I felt sure that their young leader and spokesperson must definitely suffer from some sort of disordered intellect. Or perhaps I was right and it was simply a game they were playing…but on second thoughts perhaps not. For as I paused to look back I saw that the teenage youth had called the others out of the water, where hastened by him they were hurriedly drying off on the grassy slope of the bank, reluctantly divesting themselves of wet undergarments and dressing from small dry piles of clothing.

Puzzled, still of two minds and more than a little concerned, I could only shake my head again, albeit undecidedly. But however I looked at it, that peculiar young man back there would not have been my choice as a leader—or by any means a guardian, or person in charge, however temporarily—of a party of smaller boys at a swimming-hole. No, not at all!

Except now I saw, hurrying along the ruined road from the direction of the town, a small knot of half-a-dozen people, men and women, whose demeanor even as a group appeared to exhibit something akin to my own concerns, not to mention their suspicion—but of me! And with that thought I was suddenly aware that two of the men, and even one of the three women, were carrying weapons. The two men were armed with blunderbuss-type firearms, and the oldest, tousle-haired, wildest-looking of the women carried unsheathed a long-bladed, slightly curved machete.

I didn't like the look of these people, but there was no way to avoid them. Even though I had slowed down they came on apace; and if I had turned about to run, how would that have looked? As if I was guilty of something, or perhaps that I had *intended* to be? But I had never in my life intended any harm to anyone; and anyway, as a result of my climb I was too weary to run. All of which speculation, however brief, had taken time, while my dream had seemed eager to continue. Indeed, everything had speeded up, until the little group of townspeople was almost upon me.

"Ho, stranger!" their apparent leader, the wild woman with the machete, was first to speak as the others quickly surrounded me. "One o' the town's watchmen witnessed yer approach from his station atop the wall. Strangers are scarce here in Drearish-onst-Saltsea; and visitors on foot—alone, wi' never a sign o' produce nor ware for trade or sale, and no visible means o' conveyance for neither goods nor self—scarcer still! So what do yer here? Moreover, we saw yer talkin' ter the innocents o' Drearish at their play, whose shadows are less than lavish and nothin' ter spare for such as you. Now then...how does yer answer for yer presence here?"

"I am but a wanderer," I replied, holding up my arms so that my sleeves fell down a little to reveal my wrists and something of my bare forearms—like a conjurer declaring his absence of trickery to an audience, but without a carnival magician's occasionally impudent attitude. And after a suitable pause, I continued: "Knowing nothing of this region, however, I soon found myself climbing that hill to a crest back there, and then—seeing no sign to warn me off, or informing me of my trespass and its possibly dire consequences—I simply followed this road, whose rather poor condition suggested abandonment.

"When I reached the summit and saw the town spread below me near the shore...well, to this footsore wanderer your—er, Drearish you named it?—seemed more welcoming than threatening. And as for those bathing children back there: why, it was their eldest who questioned me, and not the other way around! But if there's a reason why I should not enter your town—perhaps because it's beset by plague, or fear of an imminent invasion?—then by all means inform me of the danger; or, if you deem it necessary, simply order me on my way and I shall at once obey, for all that I am innocent of any fell intent."

"We've seen such as you before, and even questioned one or two," the fierce woman stepped closer to me. "Aye, and some o' they's shadows waned faint and shuddery in fear o' my Shinin' Lady here!" And naming her weapon, she lifted it high and shook it at me, which caused its blade to glint however dully in the humid atmosphere. "Ah, but that one's no more and his bones are buried deep, where there is no light or shade at all, at all!"

At which very moment the dismal cloud cover opened a crack, and afternoon sunlight washed the road, the group—myself included—and the fields around. The townsman closest to the angry woman, a tall, stern-looking fellow I took to be the group's counselor or figure of some authority, at once grasped her uplifted arm and swiftly, however gently pressured—or rather obliged her—into lowering her weapon; the while saying:

"Easy now, Meg! Can't you see? The sun itself guarantees his probity! A shadow sharp as his is rarely seen in Drearish-onst-Saltsea these days, with ne'er a tremble nor the leastest shiver in it—for all your Shining Lady's threat." He pointed at the buckled cobbles under my feet, the clean-edged outline of my lengthening afternoon shadow, and continued, "Would you have me unload my weapon's rusty nails on an obviously innocent wanderer—or cut him down yourself, perhaps—just because these parts are strange to him, and him to them?"

She glanced where he indicated and blinked once, twice, then hardened her glance to a scowl. "No, no—yer prob'ly right, Jon Jessop—but he *did* speak ter the children, did he not?"

At which: "Madam!" I intervened. "I beg your pardon, but as stated it was more the case that the children—their eldest at least—spoke to me! And in those baffling terms such as you and your group seem accustomed to using."

"And Meg," Jon Jessop again took up my case, however obscurely, "the little ones' shadows don't cover much ground, now do they? Be reasonable, Meg, and work it out for yourself. Even that big lad back there—why, he'd be gone in a gulp, leaving monstrous hunger unassuaged! So then, let this stranger be while we go and round up the young'uns, eh? Which according to the daily roster was our duty in the first place. For see, the clouds are rolling in again and it may rain, and the shadows all acrawl and thinning down, albeit peacefully and naturally, stretching toward the night as we concern ourselves with matters that this one seems to know nothing about...and best, perhaps, left that way, eh? So since it appears Drearish-onst-Saltsea's his destination, let's say no more of our...well, our *confusion* of manners, our apparently hostile-seeming approach to outsiders—our *difficulties?*—and let him take his chances in Drearish, eh? So then, what say all of you to that, eh?"

"Well reasoned, Jon!" Another man, small and weasel-faced, spoke up, while the rest nodded and grunted their approval of Jessop's words. "For while we're stalled here, wasting our time on this one, another in the town may even now be...well, abroad and at his business."

The difficult-seeming woman, finding her aggressive methods disputed twice over, sheathed her weapon and spat her apparent disgust into the dust of the roadside. "So be it," she growled. "But do note my objection, all of you."

And: "On you go, Sir," said the counselor or whatever he was, standing aside and waving an arm expansively in the town's direction. "May good fortune follow you, and no harm befall..." A somewhat ambiguous parting comment, but one with which I could find no fault.

And as the group moved on toward the children where the

last of them climbed from their pool back up and onto the road, I was relieved to continue on my way toward the now near-distant town...

The town. Well, as for Drearish-onst-Saltsea—though its name was somehow sour and hardly reassuring—still I was now too weary to consider asking directions from anywhere else! And I certainly was not going to find the place as deserted as first imagined; for even as I trudged toward the great gates the posse of "rostered" or designated townsfolk and their young male progeny caught up and passed me by, and I could scarcely help but observe dark-eyed, black-browed Meg still scowling at me and fondling the polished stock of her Shining Lady in its leather sheath at her hip.

While behind me, also closing with the town, other folk were coming in from the fields. These would be farm laborers, I supposed—pushing or dragging their carts laden with various vegetable staples—and all in something of a bustle, seeming almost to rush along as my dream contracted once again and a pale moon sailed high over the gloom of the ocean's misted horizon, while the first murkiness of an eerie evening almost visibly deepened...

It was as if the gloaming followed close on my heels into the town, wherein the boys and their guardian or warden townsfolk had already disappeared as yet again time contracted. But as it now became obvious to me that night in these parts fell apace, I no longer speculated regarding the concerns of the people in respect of tardy or occasionally dawdling male offspring...not that the swimmers at the pool, however odd, had seemed in any way remiss or different from their elders.

As for the farming folk, hurrying home with the produce of their fields: well it was plainly necessary that they return to town while they could still see the rutted road, and thus avoid its potholes. Such were my conclusions, anyway.

And so, putting all such thoughts to the back of my mind,

I gradually made my way through the dusky, almost empty suburbs toward the squares and thoroughfares of the town's hub, as one by one the center's many lanterns and brazier fires came flickering into smoky life. And I noted that a multitude of townsfolk—whom earlier, from a distance, had appeared less than thronging in the almost humid gloom of afternoon and early evening—were now beginning to emerge from their thatched homes and workplaces, streaming into the cobbled streets in scarcely anticipated numbers...possibly the entire community! And I concluded they could only be a night-favoring sect or clan...apparently.

By driftwood-fired braziers under the awnings of street-fronting restaurants, I inhaled the familiar aromas of roasting nuts, frying fish, warm bread and other less identifiable foodstuffs, and was suddenly hungry; a frequent occurrence in my dreams. But I breathed a sigh of relief at the feel and jingle of disturbed coinage in my pockets; currency which did not consist of the triangular tonds I had hoped for, which I would have recognized at once, but small square wedges of dull silver, worn thin and void of stamped portraits and values through much usage. However, there were plenty of these "coins," and in dreams beggars can't be choosers.

At a long table served by a thin, elderly but still agile woman in an apron, I made to seat myself until she waved me to a bench directly under a hanging lantern. "You'll see far better here, I think," she explained—and then, rather more quietly or under her breath as she followed close behind me, but not too close—"As will I..." And when I sat down where indicated she continued: "You'll excuse me, Sir, I'm sure, but I don't recognize you as a regular customer or towny? However, I could definitely use your custom!" (This last an afterthought as I deposited a pair of glinting silver squares onto the smooth scrubbed boards of the table,) "But you see...."

"No need to explain," I cut her short, "for even as a newcomer here I'm gradually becoming used to Drearish's quaint customs and, er, careful, even complicated phraseology when speaking to strangers."

"A stranger, eh?" She nodded as she gathered up my coins.

"As I correctly surmised—but not very clever of me and hardly surprising. We don't get too many casual visitors in Drearish-onst-Saltsea these days, Sir—nor nights, for that matter—but you are welcome anyway. And what can I do for you?"

"I'm hungry!" I replied, patting my empty stomach. "Which has to be fairly obvious. So if you'll be so good as to supply a menu?—or if none such exists simply to describe your delicacies—which I'm certain will be more than adequately satisfying as well as tasty…? For while I detect a tempting range of aromas from your kitchen's open door there, I fail to see anything of their sources. And so—"

But there I paused, for while other patrons were now taking their seats on benches on both sides of the long table, I momentarily glimpsed in a muttering assembly of folk, as they passed—nervously, I thought—along the street, a figure I believed I recognized: the now even more tousle-haired, and yet more wild-looking Meg of the Shining Lady! She had appeared to be staring at me—perhaps had even been following me—but was so unexpected a presence that my sighting of her was no more than that: a mere glance. And when I looked again, already she had disappeared, having lost herself in the jostling, agitated, apparently apprehensive or intimidated crowd. But… by what agency intimidated?

And: "Meg?" I must have mouthed the word, the name, quietly to myself; but the woman of the street tavern—whose hearing must be exceptional, for all her years—had indeed heard me.

"*Ah!* Meg Merrily!" she exclaimed. "Was she with that bunch? I didn't see her. But then I wasn't looking. And as for food," she abruptly changed the subject, "you may ask anyone at this table and they'll tell you that my fried fish are the best in Drearish-onst-Saltsea—or as far as the salt sea itself may reach, which is all the way to the horizon!"

"Aye, that's true!" someone seated a little further along the bench spoke up. "And Daisy uses the best dripping to fry her own recipe crispy batter, too!"

"Well, good!" I leaned forward to nod my thanks along the table for this recommendation from a youngish, smiling man who appeared to be the one praising Daisy's fried fish suppers.

For her part Daisy grinned with her few pearly white teeth and nodded, then straightened up from her slight stoop to acknowledge the accolades from others at the table. "A good big piece of fish, with battered bits to boot—and all for a single glitterslip!" she boasted. "Aye, and *twice* as good and grand for this gentleman stranger's *pair* of glitterslips! What? No cheapskate this one, and no skate at all—not at my table—but the very bestest of fresh-catched cod!"

"Which I'm sure will do nicely," I told her.

"And a slice of fresh bread to soak up the vinegar!" she chuckled, hurrying off to her kitchen and barely avoiding a thin, patently elderly—if paradoxically youngish-looking person—as he emerged from the open doorway, blocking her path if only for a moment...and in that same moment attracting my attention.

For now in a frail, stammering voice as he stumbled more readily into view, this sadly ailing creature leaned on a stick and queried: "Who is it mentioned Meg Merrily?"

"Er, that would be me," I spoke up, seeing how my voice seemingly guided him along the string of folk seated on the bench on my side of the table. "I met her just today, maybe an hour or so ago—or maybe two, what with time's strange slippage and what all—but not much more than that. She was in a group outside the wall, gathering up some children from their swimming hole."

"Aye," the youngish-old-man croaked, and awkwardly seated himself beside me, where his shadow—as faint as a shallow breath on a window—fell on the table. "She'd be a volunteer, would Meg. She usually is—and not without good cause. As for her name, Merrily: a misnomer if ever there was one—but again forgivable for all that..."

Staring into his face, I saw partly filmed eyes. He wasn't blind, not yet, but very nearly so. And because what he had said seemed to me to invite investigation, I replied: "Oh, really? Meg has a reason for being...well, so abrupt?" With which words, for the first time, and despite that I was somewhat cautious—for I had learned from many a previous dream to beware delving too deeply into secrets it were best *not* to unveil—I had almost succumbed to a temptation to explore what seemed to me a mystery here. But no, before my frail friend could reply, and before I could make any further, possibly dangerous inquiries, Daisy was back with my bread, fried fish and a small bowl of malt vinegar all on a tray...and on her withered lips a barely concealed warning:

"Billy, my poor Billy!" She put down my meal on the table, grasped Billy's thin shoulders in both hands and advised him thus: "Mention no more of such things to the gentleman, son. He's safe in the streets with all the people around, and you wouldn't want to put him off his food—now would you? Neither him nor my other customers, eh? You surely wouldn't want to frighten them all away, still unfed and hungry..."

He looked up at her, or whatever he saw of her, and replied "No, Ma. I wouldn't want to do that. For after all, your wayside business is the business by which we live...however tenuously, or even terminally, some of us. And anyway, who lends ear to anyone faint, fading and possibly foolish as me and...and mine?" Then with an audible, gulping sob: "For I'm like unto a leper or a leech, to certain of the folk in Drearish—someone or *Thing* to avoid, *lest in its turn it leeches on them!*"

But listening to the pair, I thought, "What, *son?* Did I hear her correctly? And *Ma,* did he call her Ma? Old Daisy and Billy: mother and...and a man tending toward elderly himself? Well, she was old, but not *that* old, surely? And as for Billy—a much younger man than he appeared, apparently—could he be the carrier of some weirdly mordant, ageing disease? For terms such as tenuous and terminal did seem to hint at such.

"Billy!" the woman spoke again, in aggravation. "Now see what!" She obviously referred to the fact that at least half of her would-be customers had now changed their minds and had risen to their feet, making to leave. And glaring at me, as if her problem was of my doing: "As for you, Sir—you at least should stay, if only so as not to waste my good food!"

She need not have worried; no way was I intent upon leaving! And as I set about my meal, so that handful of Daisy's customers who yet remained commenced muttering their orders, and once

again, at the trot, off went Daisy into her kitchen. As for Billy:
"I'm sorry if I disturbed you, Sir," he said, with a groan as
he climbed unsteadily to his feet. "But I have not...I've not been
well recently. Not for quite a while, in fact. Please forgive me..."
"But of course—yes, of *course!*" I reassured him. "I'm certain
you meant...meant no...meant no harm?" That last even as he
leaned closer, and whispered in my ear:
"Avoid the forest some miles to the east, Sir, the moist and
fertile woodland under the hills." Following which and before
I could question what was obviously a warning, he took up his
stick and went stumbling after his Ma, leaving a vague, strange
translucence attendant to his feet and trailing behind him...

Even as had been recommended and boasted, Daisy's fried
fish was as good if not better than in many of the eateries in
other dreamlands where I had eaten—which even included
Pazza's Pantry, a much famed restaurant in the cliff-hugging,
precipitous town of Baharna on the Isle of Oriab in an entirely
different world or dreamland, as recommended to me upon
a time by Eldin the Wanderer and his colleague David Hero,
called Hero of Dreams—and who would "dream" of doubting
endorsements such as theirs?

And finally replete and as I made to leave the table, I saw the
old woman reach up with a taper to light a lantern, until then
forgotten where it hung from a protruding sign. Unsurprisingly,
the wooden sign's slightly singed legend informed of *"Daisy's
Diner: Finest Fish & Other Foodstuffs!"* Well certainly—I could
only agree! And smiling I nodded my farewell and set off to try
and find lodgings for the night.

As for that last, however: easier said than done.

The flood of townspeople from their homes had now become
a virtual parade of recalcitrant yet apparently regular, perhaps
habitual groups of long-standing yet diffident-seeming friends
and cliquish associates—or simply get-togethers with rather
somber, indifferent neighbours—or common family gatherings

such as the party Meg Merrily had accompanied. Though who might readily accept the company of grousers such as Meg and her Shining Lady? Well…

…But then again, who could say? There must surely be reasons for her attitude, even such as old (young?) Billy had more than hinted at. And come to think of it, one or two folks *other* than Billy, at that! If not openly, then obscurely but not at all improbably.

Still, no time to ponder all that, for my dream once more seemed intent on hurrying things along. A ground mist had come up and was still writhing as it rose; and the night had grown that much darker despite its misty moon and a thin scattering of stars. Also, to my annoyance, I had somehow managed to lose myself as I wandered through what I had assumed were Drearish-onst-Saltsea's innermost streets. Oh, the centre was close by, for sure—I told myself—for arriving at various junctions I could smell the smoke and other more savoury exhalations from lanterns and braziers. But even as I entered the narrow and often winding alleys to explore the beckoning warmth and light of these scattered sources, so the deceptive muffled sounds of the aforementioned group gatherings grew fainter with distance and the light of lanterns or other nimbuses fainter still—and I lost my way yet again.

What was worse, on one or two occasions as I paused to scan all about, I thought to spy a furtive figure slipping out of sight into this or that dark doorway or similar recess. A pursuer? But who, and why chase after me? Not crazy Meg, I most fervently prayed! Oh, upon a time I'd been well able to care for myself; but I was no longer that spry youth, I certainly did not fancy my chances against a madwoman with a machete! And so, stepping out faster now, I carried on in a failing attempt to put greater distance between myself and my stalker; and turning a corner I flattened myself to a rough wall beneath a high, narrow balcony where a pair of lanterns dangled from the corners of the projecting overhang, their dull glimmer lighting the street with a welcome if spasmodic illumination. And in the next moment:

"Ho, fellow!" Came a friendly however cautious, husky voice from the darkness above the balcony, which startled me into jumping from cover out into the street. "Oh, and in a hurry, are we?" The voice continued. "I heard the echoing of your footsteps, and now the harsh panting of your breath. Are you a thief, hurrying away from the recent robbery of some poor victim...or are you yourself the victim, to display such haste? If the first, then on your way, lest I call for the thief-takers! But if the latter...then you should perhaps accept my offer of sanctuary. For only look at your sharp twin shadows, cast on the cobbles by my lanterns: how nervously they dance in the fitful light; which I take as an indication that indeed you are in danger! For this is neither a night nor district in which to be alone and lacking the comfort of companions, and I feel it would be remiss of me to leave you to your plight in this lonely, gloomy alley. What say you?"

Peering down on me from on high, the speaker's face and figure, blocked by the balcony's shelf, formed an inky blot in what feeble rays reached up to it from the dangling lanterns. And as I caught my breath and steadied my nerves, as yet failing to answer him, so his dusky silhouette turned away and made as if to go inside...only to pause as he said: "But what's this? Do I hear stealthy footsteps from around the corner?"

At which I thought to hear then too! And galvanized I quickly called out: "Sir, I would gladly accept your offer, for indeed I need lodgings for the night...and can pay for them! But how may I join you up there?"

"The door is on your right, just three paces away, set back a little in the wall," he told me. "And here's my key—catch it if you can, lest it jangle on striking the cobbles. Then, on entering, you'll find the stairs immediately to hand. But make haste, for I hear those furtive footsteps for certain now!"

Flashing silver as it twirled in air, the key fell right into my hand. At which it was as if time once again accelerated. For in mere seconds I found and was in through the door; seconds more finding me feeling my way up the dark stairs, to an unlit landing where my dark-robed rescuer ushered me through a second door into his room or rooms—also unlit. And there in those chambers I trembled in a gloom so Stygian I could make out nothing but vague outlines; such as the frame of the closed double-doors to the curtained balcony, which alone admitted light of a sort, if only the faintest glimmer from the wan moon and flickering stars

In those fast-fleeting moments as the door clicked shut behind us and my host snatched his key from my hand, it appeared he had read my mind as he exclaimed: "Ah, the light! You find yourself literally 'in the dark!' Quite so, and naturally you are unused to it, even afraid of it! But this, alas, is how *I* am obliged to survive: most of the time in darkness." And then he laughed—albeit a gurgling, phlegmy, even deranged laughter, sounding so paradoxically plaintive that it hinted of barely contained sobbing.

Sensing something of mockery or irony in his laughter—or perhaps more properly despair: an attempt at levity as a mask for pain?—I protested: "You feel obliged to dwell in darkness? Surely not, unless your obligation is utter? For why would you suffer a near permanent gloom if you don't have to? It can only be a sickness: an illness of eyes painfully sensitive to bright lights—"

"—And even daylight!" he assured me, and I sensed his nod. "Especially when the shadows of others fall stark upon the ground or wall, cast by the sun, or a lantern, or bonfire. For then…not for dear life itself would I dare venture out! But the pain is not from my eyes, from nothing physical but more a dread—an addiction: the hideous condition and complications of unavoidable need. And each time I submit, *then* the dread, the awful terror is upon me—of discovery, accusation, condemnation and lethal retribution!"

A vampire! I thought at once, and made to free myself, jerking away from him as he took my elbow and I felt his cold, cold strength. And once again—there in that darkness where slowly, so very slowly my own eyes were beginning to adjust—it was as if he read my mind:

"Ah! A creature of the night? Is that what you think of me? Well, in a way you are right, but in another quite wrong. The sun would not burn me, no—but it would reveal me! It would *define* me, my nature, the scourge that is in me, which has been forced upon me by the wicked will of another. This is the reason

I sit in my room or on my balcony, my senses alert, a weapon to hand, waiting for *him* to pass my way: the monster, the thief of thieves—*the vile and baneful shadow-man!"*

Ah, that shadow motif—again!—by now a dominant, undeniable theme in Drearish-onst-Farsea. But what did it mean? Perhaps I might finally attempt to fathom its mystery, if only to postpone whatever this madman planned for me—if indeed some weird intrigue coursed through his twisted mind. For by then I had decided that he was indeed insane!

"Your nature, and the...the *scourge* that is in you?" I repeated his thickening, increasingly viscous words even as a resolute hand transferred from my arm to my chest and applied pressure, while reeking, bitterly cold breath struck me physically in the face; agencies in combination that conspired to propel me stumblingly to the rear, until the back of my trembling legs met with an obstruction and I fell—but not far, and then only onto the seat of a creaking chair!

"The wicked will of another?" Despite my stick-dry mouth, I somehow found strength to continue speaking, once more managing to repeat his words and suffix them with a scarcely veiled suggestion of my own: "But as yet you haven't said what plagues you...haven't revealed the nature of this fearful enigma. And here I sit, your captive audience—or so it would appear— yet none the less willing to hear you out..."

For a moment he made no answer and I sensed him drawing back, if only a short pace or two, as his inky blot of a figure became a slender, slightly softer silhouette on the jet-black backdrop of a chamber that seemed less gloomy now; where little by little—but oh so slowly—my eyes were adapting to the tenebrous lack of light. And finally he spoke:

"It can do no harm to explain my...my condition. Indeed, it may relieve something of the burden it puts on me, which even now compels my every action, counseling me not to...well, not to delay! But since you strike me as an intelligent, apparently selfless, indeed guileless and—how shall we put it?—'charitable if gullible' sort of fellow—perhaps when all is known you may even take pity on me and put aside any remaining reluctance... except I very much doubt it. But there again..."

His voice had lowered, becoming ominously guttural toward the end of an analysis which in the main appeared to censure me, but nevertheless seemed introspective. Until at last—after a silent but nerve-rending pause—abruptly he appeared to have balanced accounts, the status quo prevailing as the picture he had painted of me won the day, and in a somewhat lighter tone he continued:

"Very well, then. Let me explain something of myself— which is to say, my *condition*." And taking a moment to order his thoughts, while stirring the darkness and shattering the silence as he dragged a second chair gratingly into position facing me, he seated himself as if to commence his story.

But before that:

"I should warn you," he said, "that my weapon is still to hand—is actually *in* my hand—which as stated is not so much a threat as a warning. For no, I have no desire, none whatever, to actually *kill* you! And you may believe this or not, but my only desire is the *preservation* of life, my own uppermost…well, for what that's worth. For with this *addiction* working so powerfully within me, I am forced to continue activating the horror and indulging myself again, and again, and yet again! And so, in the event you should think to act foolishly against me in an attempt to deny me a very necessary however horrifying habit—alas, I would be driven to kill you!"

At which I assured him: "Such a thought—to act against you—has not entered my head!" Which was true, as of that moment at least. For with time on the move again there had been little enough of it in which to think my situation through! And in answer to what he must surely have considered a coward's submission:

"Very well, then," his outline nodded. And in another moment of fast-fleeting time:

"This entire house was and is my home. And as a man who preferred his own company, and within bounds exclusively, I was usually entirely on my own and pleased to be left that way. I lived alone, stocked my pantry but rarely, prepared my food additionally from a good-sized, high-walled vegetable garden to the rear of the house, washed my own clothes, purchased wood for my fire in the winter, and when aught else was needed ventured out as briefly as possible to shop for my requirements.

"Too relieve my boredom, when beset by self-imposed loneliness—also to avoid becoming entirely, helplessly housebound—I occasionally went out for exercise, walking lonely miles to pick mushrooms in a forest under the hills, or enjoying local comestibles and the gossip of whichever eateries I patronized. On similarly rare occasions I also attended Saltsea's regular carnivals, fairs, markets and masques, and such, whether original to Saltsea or brought in by itinerant players. Why, to a certain extent I even accepted the irritation and annoyance of the brats who rough-and-tumbled, frisking in the streets and fairgrounds! But still I was known as the town's recluse: an oddly familiar, rarely seen yet recognizable figure; but known only for my solitary, unsociable nature. Just an estranged old fool, but never a threat—indeed incapable of harm...

"Ah, but Saltsea was a different place in those days, all of fifteen...but no, wait!—even twenty!—or yet *more* years ago!—when I was a different person. But different only in one sense, for since then I have become more...well, shall we say, *more* capable?

"But all those years speeding by, here in Drearish-onst-Saltsea where chronology is less than constant and anything but synchronous—the longer their years, the shorter their days—and, putting it briefly, where time seems illogical to them that age, others who don't, apparently, and at least one who has no say in the matter but does as he must in whatever opportunities our temporal impermanence allows him—meaning myself.

"Ah! But there, I have strayed however briefly. Forgive me and I'll continue...

"The shadow-man was a carnival worker, a roustabout who lured townsfolk into spending their glitterslips on alleged 'games of chance' and salacious peepshows, or worthless 'magical' trinkets forged in base metals, and many another such swindle. Despite which...well, who would have suspected him of dastardly criminality, this bravo with his colorful, bellowing language and cajoling, whispered invitations to enter the tasseled tents of lewd and tattooed but otherwise naked ladies? For these enticements were by no means viewed as crimes, but would later be excused and laughed over in the alehouses—by both victims and onlookers alike!—as simple amusements, a jester's drolleries, the glibly facile clownishness of a mountebank...but never as the disguise and preparations of an occasional murderer and thief. Well, a thief of sorts...

"As for cunning: aye, *as a fox*, this one, on whom to this day I plan vengeance! Why, his chosen cover was the carnival itself, in which he first arrived in Saltsea; which was the town's one and only name at that time. Ah, and what a disguise, a hidey-hole the carnival was! For if he left his vile practice till late in the final night, when the trappings were being removed, taken down before the carny's departure, and then if he got too greedy...why, there would be no suspicious party to investigate when his deed was discovered—if ever! Which in my case it was not. He took what he took from me, but left me alive, and went on his way..."

Despite my predicament, I was at this point so intrigued that I could not resist an urge to interrupt this dark creature's narrative. But it was only when I spoke that for the first time I felt something of an unsuspected lethargy, a creeping weariness in my every organ, bone and even my speech—my entire being. "He took what he took, you say, but still you haven't said what *it was* that he took!"

"Eh?" Startled, he sat up straighter in his chair. "What? You've not guessed it? Haven't you been listening? Or have you perhaps been thinking certain dire thoughts? What's more, suddenly I detect activity, groping motions! Must I remind you of my earlier warning, which cautioned you against unseemly, possibly hostile activity?"

"I have of course been listening!" I quickly replied, fumbling numbly in a pocket for my pipe and matches. "And your story is fascinating, but it would seem my concentration is failing. My mind is much given to wandering, and I have found that without my pipe I have some difficulty focusing."

"Ah! Your pipe!" He relaxed somewhat, sinking back down a little in his chair. "Then I shall reduce the precautionary pressure on my trigger finger while you light your pipe. But try to move carefully, my friend, very carefully. Then, in the brief but flaring light from your lucifer, and in answer to your insipid complaint, you may see for yourself something of my *condition,* my remedy, and the evil my tormentor worked upon me that time in his maze of warped mirrors..."

As he paused I struck a long-life match, especially designed for the lighting of pipes, but was trembling so much I don't know how I managed to suck the flame down into the bowl! My terror had been greatly amplified by his words and his voice, which was now at its most glutinous. But somehow I ceased my shivering and kept still as I beheld what the hissing radiance of my match revealed.

And because I had initiated the act, I instinctively, automatically carried it on and actually succeeded in lighting my pipe before thrusting the now full-flaring match out before me, more surely illuminating the phenomenon taking place within that room.

It was the shadows, aye—mine and what ought to have been his. Except mine was reaching out writhingly across the boarded floor, *denying* the flame which should have thrust it back, away from my hideous host—*whose face and form were now revealed, but* without *shadows of their own!*

His hideous face, yes, which as my shuddering, reluctantly extruding and utterly misshapen shadow continued to leak out and away from me—or to be *absorbed* into him?—now appeared to be extending its stain up into that face, revealing the rapidly deepening shapes and shadows of those ghastly snow-white features: his long, hooked nose, pale pouting lips, bushy eyebrows and barely opaque lids over deeply sunken, scarlet orbs whose gaze bored hypnotically into me!

And now I knew—and he *knew* I knew—why he waited to trap the being he had called the shadow-man: a once-human creature who had stolen his shadow, just as he was now attempting to steal mine!

But attempting? No, he was succeeding! And as I tried to jump to my feet—only to fall back into my chair when my legs failed me—so he too made to stand up, and again succeeded. Indeed he *snatched* himself up, skeletally thin and pale, but swiftly darkening, *filling in!* For even as I felt weaker and less than substantial, so *his* lineaments, his wan form in general, took on a visible penumbra: an as yet incomplete image only a little less than an actual shadow. But *my* shadow continued to shrink, thinning out as it trickled blackly across the floor and far less hesitantly, in fact irresistibly, up into him!

Then, as my long match finally flickered, even as it began to burn my quivering fingers, so *my* shadow-man threw off his cloak in a strangled cry of triumph, but also of distress and weird misery:

"I did not want to do this!" he cried. "You must believe me! Even though I lied to you, I didn't *want* to destroy you utterly… but my need is such that I have no choice…especially now that you know all. *Yes*, that devil stole my shadow, there in his terrible tent, but he did not take it all. Perhaps he was disturbed by other townies seeking cover, when beyond his lair's canvas flap it started to rain? But I have never fully known the devil's reason for sparing me, not for sure—only the fact that he didn't take it all! He might have been tempted, I suppose, but it has been said that a man's shadow is but an image of himself, his psyche or spirit-of-mind, without which he is nothing, not only soulless but dead! If he had killed me, what then when the townsfolk found my dead, empty body—a corpse without a shadow? He would have been revealed, apprehended and put an end to. And so he took only half of what was needed. And at first, as I failed to understand what had happened to me, numb in body and mind, I simply staggered from his tent into the rain and returned home soaking wet but more or less…well, actually very *much* less…indeed barely intact!

"In the rain and sullen light of evening I had little or no shadow, but then neither had anyone else. So, all thanks to the weather, no one noticed—including me. I was only aware of how tired I felt, exhausted; but not of how my vitality, and something of my soul and life itself, had been stolen by that near-hypnotic beast—even as I am now stealing yours! But of course that knowledge would come soon enough: indeed the very next morning, with the sunrise. The sun, yes, and the strong black shadows which it should have painted upon the earth; which in fact it did...except for mine! And with that came the awful realization and inevitable acceptance of my ... of my *transition*. And I was so lucky, for no one saw me hurrying to get back inside my house again, that morning...

"You wonder at my use of those words: 'my transition'? Well, such it was—for I had become a shadow-man, and more solitary and secretive than ever! Aye, and something inside me told me things would be different for me from now on, for already I could feel the urge, the beginning of my addiction, taking hold of me. And it were better, I think—as so often I have indeed thought—had he sucked me dry completely that night, and killed me outright..."

"Ah, but you—" the creature had barely paused, his voice grown even stronger, more hurried and passionate now—"you are fortunate, for you will not be alone...never alone, bricked up with the others in the walls of my dark cellar...for I *can't* let you live, not now...not as one who knows...who has learned what a liar and a monster I am! But as you can now see for yourself, I have not lied in the telling of my story..."

Like me, my brave match was almost ready to give up the ghost, but Drearish's freakish opposition to matters chronological— such as the speed of time and synchronicity's affinity with coincidence—had returned and was for the moment prevailing: the former slipping yet more speedily, smoothly by as the *miss-matched* latter skittered and *my* match burned on and on. And even as I surrendered to the pain and tried to fumble that last half-inch of matchstick and its precious flame away from my agonized fingertips, then—even immobilized, anchored by horror to my chair—I began to believe, to understand, that all of this was real and might actually anticipate the end of my dream...or perhaps the end of everything, and more especially of me!

What, the end of me? Like those other victims bricked up in this maniac's cellar? How many victims, I wondered? And why was old-young Billy not one of them?

But no, *my* shadow-man had not killed the prematurely decrepit son of Daisy, else right now and obviously Billy were no longer a barely corporeal specter in the care of his mother but more likely a shriveled thing bricked up in a cellar's nitrous wall! Furthermore, it also seemed unlikely that Billy had suffered his *depletion* during a visit to a roustabout's "Maze of Mirrors" or some other such "amusement," but far more plausibly that his fate had been organized to occur in a spot farther afield—for example a forest under the hills, where the mushrooms grow—lest the townies quickly develop a nagging doubt, a growing suspicion of itinerant carnivals! Moreover, in Billy's case…well, he obviously had not yet discovered how best to preserve himself at the odious expense of others; but despite that, small wonder even now that normal or conventional folk should tend to consider it wise to avoid him "like a leech," and one which eventually might commence leeching on them!

All of this introspection—aided by time's slippage—racing helter-skelter through my mind; along with the knowledge that I, too, was a victim, and very close to the end of my tether, my wits, my own terrified, shrinking shadow! Yet even ravaged and weak as I was, still I was able, albeit frantically, deliriously, to consider escape. For I had to face it: escape or evasion—some miraculous avoidance of my fate, resulting in deliverance from this exultant yet seemingly irresolute, paradoxically mournful shadow-man-*thing* standing naked before me—were the only remaining, barely possible eventualities, worthy of consideration!

More aware of my surroundings now, with my eyes somewhat adjusted to the room's gloom, I gazed at his arms and bowed legs—like spindly sticks with knobby joints at elbows and wrists, knees and ankles—but also at the yawning funnel-mouth of his powerful looking blunderbuss, a weapon no longer pointed at me but dangling from the parchment hand and long, sharp-nailed fingers that held it.

Also his body: skeletal yes, but no longer pale and thin as water, where each rib stood out over its freshly formed shadow;

and dark-cushioned nipples like tiny pustules adorned the flat plates of his chest; and the bones of his shoulders, looking likely to explode at any moment out through his stretched, darkening skin. Stretched, darkening and throbbing, yes—with the weight and pressure of *my* once-shadow!

And all the time my essence, my soul, what remained of that shadow of mine, continuing to leak across the floor in a thin black stream, to be siphoned up into his starved muscles and brittle bones. It was monstrous, loathsome, an abomination; and even as he shrieked, so did I as finally my match expired where it stuck to my scorched fingers, and I found strength from somewhere to hurl my pipe at my tormented torturer, and also to lurch like a deranged, stiffly crumpling cripple from my chair to grapple however feebly with his bony arm and the spider-like hand that held his blunderbuss!

And again he shrieked—but not in rage! And once more I joined in, for I thought that the sudden blaze of blinding light could only come from the fires of Hell wherein I had been plunged as I died. But what of the sound of some door's splintering? The door to Hell? What, a *wooden* door, and fragile? I thought not! And I was by no means dead; and the shadow-man was *still* raging as he fought back, trying to thrust me away from where I clung to him!

And face to face he screamed accusingly at me: "Damn you! *Damn you!* I took back my key, but when you came in from the alley you failed to lock the oaken door behind you!"

My attack and everything else that was happening had thrown the fiend off balance. And now our struggles were spinning us about, allowing me to see that this abrupt, unanticipated light that was scattering the shadows in that bleak and spartan room was from a flaring faggot; a brand in the hand of a wild figure of whom I felt certain that no one in Drearish—and certainly not I—could have failed to recognize.

For it was Meg—Meg Merrily—who now rushed upon the shadow-man, letting fall her torch in favour of her Shining Lady. My pursuer Meg, who had tracked me suspiciously, unerringly through the night streets of Drearish-onst-Saltsea; my rescuer now, liberator and deliverer from evil!

The fallen torch's incandescent materials had scattered across the floor, making a path of fire of the resinous floorboards; a path which seemed to extend directly to the balcony's curtains and at once set them ablaze. And as finally my shrieking adversary hurled me away, so his efforts must have caused him to apply pressure inadvertently to the trigger of his weapon. With an awesome roar the great blunderbuss fired its load harmlessly into the flaking plaster of the ceiling, but the stunning sound was sufficient in itself at close quarters to hurl me back into my chair, from which I could do no more but follow the final acts in that chaotic sequence of events.

I saw Meg's Shining Lady—shining now in an arc of golden firelight and terrible vengeance—reaching up high as she sprang to an attack on the shadow-man. And as the heavy curved blade paused above him, and the spindly monster backed off from it, so Meg howled her revenge:

"I've waited long and long, you hell-spawned thing—but I knew I'd get yer sooner or later. First of all for Zhak, who loved me from a child, sawed logs for all the folks against the chill o' winter, and vanished one bleak, black night without rhyme or reason while makin' his rounds. His cart was found, still loaded with logs, close to the town's center, but never a sign of Zhak. So then, first for him, and second for myself: upon a time a bonny lass, now changed forever by you to a hateful, vengeful hag!"

And backing up tearfully to a blazing wall, the shadow-man howled back at her: "Aye, do it, Meg, *do it!* For as my guilty, regretful tears are witness, I too have waited long and long!"

At which Meg's lusting machete thundered down on him, and his skull split open, and his brains spattered yellow as the yolk of a shattered egg! But even as he flopped and fluttered spastically down the wall, so Meg yanked her ghastly weapon free of his hinged skull, swung it hard and struck again—and his sundered head on its gaping neck sprang free.

"But as for you—" She now turned to me as once more I lurched up and out of my chair. "—I owes yer an apology, for I heard just enough o' how things were before I burst in the door." She reached out a trembling hand to me, only pausing as she saw that she still held the reeking machete.

And: "*Ugh!*" Meg gasped then, as if she had never seen her weapon before, then threw the thing down with such force that its point pierced and got fixed in a blazing floorboard, where it stood upright, wedged in position. She gazed at it there—wonderingly, I thought, but with eyes suddenly confused, mystified—blinking in the light of the now quickening fire.

I too gazed, at first unbelievingly, as my eyes took in and my brain gradually accepted what Meg seemed not to have noticed: the anomalous shadows on the floor—more especially the one laid down by me—its black, thinly recalcitrant stream flowing across the smoking floorboards *in reverse* to where, despite its deficiency of texture and vitality, it was being absorbed through my insensible feet, legs and torso into my aching sensorium, where indeed I sensed it settling as with a sigh!

Still black, yes, what remained of that curtailed shadow of mine—but a very different colour where it was repulsed by the lolling, decapitated corpse and expanding pool of the cadaver's emissions! And pointing a shuddering finger at the monster seated with his back to the wall: "Meg!" I tried to shout over the roar of the now blazing fire. "Look at his shadow! Do you see that ghastly thing's shadow?"

Looking where I pointed and nodding, she replied however vaguely, "Aye, but we must leave now." And tugging at my arm, repeating herself to emphasize her intention: "We must leave *now*—or stay and burn alongside him!"

"But his shadow…" I began to insist. "It—"

"—Is *not* a shadow!" she told me, dragging me stumbling to the door's shattered panels where they hung in their frame. "Shadows are dry and black, my friend—*not wet and red!*" And finally as we fled to the stairwell: "Nor are they normally faint and a wispy grey, like yours is now!"

Meg agreed to see me safely to the town's main gate, along a lonely, tortuous back-street route that was mainly devoid of lanterns. And as we walked we talked:

"Not only should I apologize," she said while assisting me along the way, "but you have my most sincere thanks.

For without yer chance entry into Drearish-onst-Saltsea my hardened heart would yet weigh as a monstrous fossil, washed out from the sea-cliffs by a stormy ocean's swirl. But now I walk with a light step, almost as a girl, and since I am not yet a crone perhaps time will so slow down for me that I may once more take on a girlish mien! My Zhak is long gone, alas—and who can say whereunto?—but he would not have me livin' alone and lonely. At least I don't think so. This ring he gave me was forever—" She showed me its dull gleam upon her finger—"and I gave him its twin…" She fell silent for a moment, but then said:

"As for you, Sir…why, I don't even know your name!"

"Call me Jon, or Allain, or whatever you will," I replied. "I have no name as yet, at least not in this strange land of dreams, from which—and forgive me for saying so—I would be very glad to depart; and that despite that as yet I haven't even taken to myself a dream-name in these parts!"

"Understood," she nodded curtly. "And I can't blame yer for anticipatin' an early departure. So then…where will you go?"

"I can't say," I shook my head. "Perhaps a place where the people have little or no interest in the density of a man's shadow!" And frowning, I went on: "Except…it's very odd, I know, but I keep feeling this strange sensation, a kind of personal permanence, a reluctant acquaintance with disagreeable surroundings—as of belonging here, but against my will—and that's a sensation I don't much care for."

"Also understood," she replied, and once again her nod. "But I'm sorry now that I stood on that landin' listenin', and didn't burst the door in just a moment or two sooner. But know this, Jon or Allain, or whatever I will: if ever yer need a friend, shelter, food, a voice in yer favour—Meg Merrily will always be here for you."

I thanked her warmly and we parted just outside the gate, watched over by someone on the great wall overhead. But before I let her go: "Meg, about Zhak…"

She looked at me curiously, frowningly. "Aye?"

"Back there we left a house in flames, but its cellars should be intact. When the embers have cooled, look for Zhak there…" And when her mouth fell open I went on: "You'll find remains,

Meg—quite a few, perhaps—but if by chance they're Zhak's, you'll know them from his ring."

Then, without another word she was gone.

And me, too, despite my weariness, my loneliness, into the night...

Since when I've wandered afar, spent many a restless night in that dream where Drearish-onst-Saltsea—or perhaps just Saltsea now, who can say?—became a nightmare; which, like a fading shadow, has slipped little by little from my memory as most dreams are wont to do, until by now I should have forgotten it entirely. But no, my shadow, or its absence is always there (or not?) to remind me.

Moreover, my visit to Drearish that time, however brief, has left me with a companion legacy no less weird than being shorn of a worthy shadow. Simply put, I have lost the ability to rouse myself up into the waking world! I dream on and on, and in many a dream-world—some well known to me and others entirely strange—I experience dreams within dreams, endlessly. And even if I did awaken, how would I fare with a weakened body, a withered soul, and a shadow as faint as a dying breath? Or would everything I've lost be returned somehow to me?

Last night I slept, and this morning woke up in Ulthar: a place I know well enough and better than most of the many dreamlands that I've only partly-explored; and now I think I know what must be done and who might help me to do it. I shall seek the advice of Kuranes in Celephais, or Hero and Eldin, or better still a kindly old wizard named Nyrass of Theelys, who calls the latter pair of champion ruffians his friends! And if none of these can help me, then I'll just have to accept that the waking world of my birth is dead to me—or perhaps that I am dead in the waking world!

Only one thing for certain: my shadow may be weak but my will is not. And though I may feel an occasional strange *urge*...I shall throw myself down from a high place rather than let that urge become an addiction. However, dead or alive (but never addicted,) there's still much to be seen and done in the dreamlands—and my shadow won't have been much of a loss to the Earth's blue seas, green fields and fertile soils—and in any case, in the darkness six feet *under* those fertile soils…

…Why, there is no light and so no shadows at all! But however things may go, by all means wish me luck!

IN DUBLIN'S FAIR CITY

A NECROSCOPE® STORY

And once again: Location, Location. Time to move on, girl...

Harry Keogh, the Necroscope, had taken the Möbius route to Dublin, Ireland. Still searching for Brenda, the once-beloved wife who had fled him when he suffered his change (for upon a time Harry had been Alec Kyle; which is to say his current body and mind had belonged to Alec Kyle, where now the mind and soul were Harry's while the body was not...or not quite.) Also which, when Kyle's body had first accommodated Harry, the result had seemed such a weird adaptation that Brenda had not been able to accept it as her husband.

Now, however, and however astonishingly, the Necroscope was gradually reforming—or shall we say conforming, transforming, morphing?—into a semblance, avatar or amalgam which Brenda might find more agreeable. For indeed Harry himself had accepted that, however strange the change, he now looked more like *him*, the man he had once been, despite that his initial or original embodiment had "died" in a firefight in a Russian fortress some years ago. So perhaps if Brenda saw him now things might be different between them; perhaps she would more readily accept him as the "real" Harry Keogh.

All of which to explain, however insufficiently, why the Necroscope, the man who could converse with the Great Majority—the grateful dead, who were his friends and would care for him in any way possible—was now in Dublin; for he remembered several occasions when Brenda had mentioned that as very small child she had been with her parents visiting an elderly relative in Ireland, the single visit she had ever made to Dublin however fondly she recalled it. So even as history is said to repeat, it seemed possible that Dublin was where she had gone, taking their infant boy child with her.

She had mentioned a place on the outskirts of the city, a place of parks, sheltering trees, wooden benches, and winding old streets; part of the ancient Dublin to which Harry had now taken himself. But although he arranged lodgings of only four days at the small hostelry in the antique suburbs, by the third evening Brenda remained unknown and even unheard of by any of the numerous exanimate persons in the well-tended local graveyard. For of course Harry had checked on her whereabouts first with the Great Majority, who would have been aware of the fact if Brenda had come among them.

But that third summer night as the Necroscope lay in his bed in an oak-beamed garret room with a single small window that opened outward on the soft air over a narrow cobbled street, he did hear something. Nothing to do with Brenda, but a female voice and sweet all the same, it reminded him of a refrain he had known from his childhood in a boys' school in the colliery village where he'd been raised from a child to a youth, mainly alone in the land of the living but with a great many friends among those who were no longer living. Part of a sad little song, he'd always thought it, yet a song so strong in its pathos and so easy on the ear and in the mind that it wasn't at all hard to remember. This one small part was simply the cry of a street vendor in the night, which seemed strange in itself until Harry realized that the voice was reaching him on the deadspeak ether, his unique telepathic link with the dead. At which he began to rouse himself a little more fully from the edge of sleep.

A-live a-live O! A-live a-live O!—sang the voice. And: *cockles and mussels, alive a-live O!*

In his drowsiness and scarcely aware that he did it, Harry began to answer that faint sad cry in the night:

"In Dublin's fair city, where the girls are so pretty
I first set my eyes on sweet Molly Malone,

As she wheeled her wheelbarrow through streets broad and narrow,
Crying cockles and mussels alive a-live O!"
The sweet voice in the night had fallen silent at once, indeed at the very first deadspeak note from the Necroscope's mouth and metaphysical mind. But now she spoke:

Oh? And who be that, then? Just another fool mockin' me? Well if so Oi should warn ye: them that mocks Molly gets cursed by Molly, an' for all that ye're dead it's a very hurtful curse Oi'll call down on ye! So then, on ye're way now and leave Oi in peace...

More fully awake now, Harry had to smile at her spirit, her threatened malediction, and yet more surely her charming Irish brogue, but he did his best to keep such amusement to himself. "Molly?" he said. "Is it really you, Molly Malone?"

Well o'course it's Oi! She snapped back. *Who else would it be, walkin' the streets an' callin' out me wares, like Oi always did when Oi had a body, an' veins in me body, an' blood in me veins...aye, an' shellfishy wares Oi could sell to the livin', be they good wares or not-so-good wares or not-nearly-so-good wares. So then, that's me an' it's the truth. But Oi'll ask ye again: who be ye? It's strange but ye feel...warm? Now that's somethin' Oi never did feel before, not here in the darkness, anyway! In fact, Oi never felt a thing!*

"No," said Harry, "I don't for a moment suppose you did. But since it's the utter darkness of death of which you're speaking: the darkness of total immobility, inanimation—in short, the cold and darkness of the tomb—that's hardly surprising." His words seemed cold even to Harry himself, but their delivery was soulful and heartfelt.

Oh, it's all o' what ye've said right enough, she replied, her voice hushed to a deadspeak gasp now. *All that an' more! For now Oi also sees a light—a flickerin' like a wee candle's flame! Or Oi think Oi sees it, or Oi fancy Oi sees it. Is it ye, stranger? Is that all ye are? A wee, warm glow an' a kindly voice in the long, long night?*

"No, I'm more than that," said Harry, with a shake of his

head that he knew she would sense. "You may have heard of me from others in your darkness; or maybe not, because I've never been this way before. But I'm Harry Keogh, known by the dead as the Necroscope—those of the dead who actually know me, anyway. But word sometimes travels slowly, which is just as well for I can't be everywhere at once!"

Again he heard her deadspeak gasping, a sound strange as strange could be coming from Molly's close-packed crumbling grave in a beggar's cemetery on the far side of the city, for in that grave there was no air to breathe and no lungs to breathe it anyway, just the calcifying bones of the long dead Molly and a few cockle and mussel shells that folks had thrown in with her at the burial. But then:

Harry Keogh, the Necroscope, she said. *Aye, an' Oi have indeed heard o' ye once or twice, but don't ask Oi when for it's hard to tell the time in this place, neither the day, year nor even the decade! But ye're more recent than historic, that much Oi may tell ye; though surely ye know it already.*

"A bit of old Irish, that!" said Harry, smiling. But his smile quickly turned to a frown. And: "Molly," he went on, "you mentioned your wares, the cockles and mussels that you sold from your barrow…"

Aye, an' the occasional crab an' lobster, too, she replied, but warily Harry thought. *What of it?*

"But you said that you sold them 'be they good wares or not-so-good wares or not-nearly-so-good wares.' Now what did you mean by that?"

For a moment Molly was silent, then in a softer, quieter tone said: *Ye may have heard somethin' o' Oi's faether, too. He were also a fishmonger an' sold his wares from a barrow.*

"Indeed I have heard of him," the Necroscope replied. "Also of your Ma. For they're in your song too, however briefly."

And he continued:

"She was a fishmonger, and sure it's no wonder,
 For so were her mother and father before…"

But Molly stopped him right there, with:

First things first, Harry: that's not *Oi's song! It may be*

*about Oi, but Oi don't recognize it. Oi don't accept the truth o'
it. Whoever made it up—put it into words—may have thought
he were doin' Oi a favour; but the whole truth, good, bad or
indifferent would have suited Oi far better. That damned song—
excuse Oi's French—leaves far too much to the imagination.*

The Necroscope was taken aback, baffled. "In what way? It
all sounds clear enough to me."

*No, it gives the wrong impression—or rather, it lacks some
very important details, fails to enlarge on certain matters—tends
to leave a listener in doubt as to...as to—well, let's just say it
leaves a person undecided.*

"You think the song fails to represent your true image?
Perhaps you'd appreciate it more if it didn't dwell so heavily on
your...your sweetness? I mean, how could you be so sweet after
all the hard work you must have put into trundling your wares
through those streets broad and narrow? Work like that must
have been very tough on you. And then there's your death from
the fever; I suspect that must mean the plague, or an epidemic of
some sort. And I would hazard a guess that it must have taken
you at a very young age, and—"

And say no more! She cried. But then, just a moment later,
with what was apparently a complete change of heart: *Oh, very
well. Why should Oi care after all this time, eh? Go on then,
Harry. Sing the next verse an' Oi'll try to explain my problems
with it, so Oi will.*

And the Necroscope responded with:
"She died of a fever and no one could save her,
And that was the end of sweet Molly Malone,
Now her ghost wheels her barrow,
Through streets broad and narrow,
Crying cockles and mussels alive a-live O!"

An' there ye have it, said Molly, sighing a deadspeak sigh.
*Right there in that one verse, tree—er, that'll be three to ye—tree
reasons, examples, o' why Oi's not at all happy with it. An' ye're
right, that word 'sweet' is one o' them.*

Still baffled, or even more so, Harry said, "You're against the word sweet? But surely that means of a lovely appearance, or a pleasant-nature, or both."

Aye, in yere world for sure, she replied. *But in mine it could have another meanin' entirely. As in a juicy piece o' fruit, for example.*

Harry frowned as he pondered the meaning of that last, but she had quickly continued:

As for this 'fever' thing. There were no plague when Oi were taken, neither plague nor epi—er, epi—

"Epidemic?" The Necroscope helped her out. "Which means a terrible contagion that rages across entire regions!"

Nothin' o' the sort, she nodded an uncompromising deadspeak nod. *Not when Oi took ill, anyway. What's more, Oi never even heard o' that word before, even though Oi caught somethin' o' its meanin' from the way ye said it. So then, Epidemic, no...Ah, but there are fevers an' there are fevers, Harry!*

At which the Necroscope believed he was beginning to understand.

An' then there's that other thing, Molly continued. *Oi mean that streets broad an' narrow thing. Well, it's true enough, there were broad streets in Dublin in Oi's day, an' narrow ones, too.*

"Still are," said the Necroscope.

Aye, but now think o' broad as in broad-minded! Molly urged. *An' narrow as in narrow-minded! Did ye not know that in Oi's day many a so-called 'street vendor' was nothin' more than a common tart, a 'sweet'-bodied whore? Sweet, aye—but often as not more than a wee bit sour, too. Never an epidemic, still it killed many a lusty young man—not to mention more than a few o' them street vendors, too. It was their so-called 'wares' that killed 'em—even as much the same thing were what killed Oi!*

"Ah!" Harry gasped, as understanding—as he saw it— suddenly dawned. "That fever you died of was...it was..." But he couldn't say or even think it, not even to himself, let alone to Molly, and so he kept the awful thought—venereal disease—to himself. No matter, for in any case she knew what had given him pause. And:

There now, said Molly with a satisfied nod, her argument justified. *So now ye see why Oi can't trust that song. Why Oi hates it an' them among the dead what tries to sing it to Oi from time to time…because it far too often gives the wrong impression and leaves Oi's reputation in doubt when people misin—er, misint—*

"When they misinterpret it?" said Harry.

Aye, that too…Oi think, Molly agreed, with typically Irish ambiguity. *They misinterpret it—just like you did less than a minute ago! Even you, Harry Keogh, mistakin' virtue for vice an' innocence for immorality!*

"But you just said that you too died of—"

No! He sensed the vehement shake of her head. *Oi said it were Oi's wares that killed Oi. But where those whores were vendors o' their not-so-sweet bodies, Oi's were the cockles an' mussels in Oi's wheelbarrow!*

Again the Necroscope gasped, as this time he recognized the truth for certain. "You were selling poisoned shellfish!?"

Oh, it's true, so it is! Molly was beginning to sob now, however quietly. *But Oi swear Oi Didn't know the harm in it until Oi, too, fell sick o' that killin' mussel fever!*

Harry nodded, frowned and queried: "Your mussels weren't fit for eating, yet you didn't know it? I'm not doubting you, Molly, but that in itself raises a question. I mean, surely you must have had some previous experience of the quality of your wares?"

Oh, Oi did, she replied, as she barely managed to control her sobbing. *But ye see, it was Oi's faether, me Da, what led me astray. An' maybe me poor old Ma too.*

And the Necroscope remembered:

She was a fishmonger, and sure 'twas no wonder,
For so were her father and mother before,
Who both wheeled their barrows,
Through streets broad and narrow,
Crying cockles and mussels alive a-live O!

"Your parents led you astray?" he said then. "Are you saying that your father sent you out to sell shellfish knowing full well they were unfit for consumption and might poison whoever ate them?"

Let me explain how it were, she said then. And after taking a moment to regain a little control over her emotions:

Those were desperate times, Harry. It was a very cold winter; there was little or no work for the men folk, an' next to nothin' by way o' wages for those few lucky ones who managed to hold on to their jobs. Money? Hah! *Precious little o' that in this entire, Godforsaken land! No, none at all, at all. No money to buy warm clothin' for small cold bodies, nor decent food for hungry families! So people were starvin'. But enough—that should set the scene for ye.*

Oi's parents were good folks, Oi shall always believe that. An' Oi blame me faether's big mistake on the simple fact that he was a good, kindhearted man. He couldn't bear the sight o' skinny little children shiverin' as they begged for scraps o' food. An' so he piled yesterday's shellfish on Oi's barrow and sent Oi out into those streets broad an' narrow. An' he told Oi: Sell them if ye can, an' if ye can't then give 'em away. An' meanwhile we'll pray there's no real harm comes o' all this, neither to us nor to them poor 'uns out there in the cold.'

Now, just lookin' at all those shiny black mussels Oi knew there were a big problem here. Because for every half-a-dozen or so o' them bivalves that were clamped tight shut, there was at least one whose shells were open a crack—like it were gaspin' for breath, which o' course it weren't—but which meant that the wee creature inside the shell were either sick or dyin' or already dead o' some sea sickness o' its own! An' as ye've said, Harry, the sick ones weren't fit for the eatin', not at all, at all. But because o' the money situ...er, situ—

"Situation," said Harry.

That too, answered the Irish in Molly, as she continued: *Because no one had any money, Oi's Da must have decided that takin' a chance on the mussels were better than lettin' folks waste away an' die o' starvation. An' he probably figured that if there were deaths among Oi's customers, we could always put the blame on hunger or the freezin' weather—though God knows he would have suffered the guilt o' it on his conscience, no less than it were on Ois, for ever. Aye, an' Oi still suffers from it, so Oi do!*

"But you did eat of your own wares," said Harry, he hoped in mitigation. "You did run the same grim risk—the same hazard— that you offered your poor customers with every sick mussel. And you did it...what, deliberately? In order to ease your own guilt and maybe something of your folks' too, especially your Da's? But did he—or they—well, get away with it? I mean, were they ever found out, and if so were they shown to be innocent or guilty? Or was the truth never discovered at all? Because in that song we hear very little of them."

There were deaths, o' course there were, she replied. *But it were when Oiself started to suffer that they left Oi with friends an' moved on—to London, Oi believe—an' good luck to them. But as far as Oi knows, the truth o' it never did come out, an' by now for sure they're dead an' gone—oh, a hundred years ago an' more, to be sure—Oi's poor old Ma an' Da! Oi did have hopes they might try to contact me some time, but that hasn't happened.*

Harry nodded. "It's only recently," he explained, "that the Great Majority have been able to contact One another—which is pretty much down to me, I believe. Because in your time, Molly, there was no Necroscope, and the dead lay quiet in their graves. So I think they must have moved on, your folks, and not just to London."

Moved on? Molly was at once curious. *Oi think Oi may have heard whispers o' such a thing: how sometimes us dead 'uns move on. But...where to?*

"To a better place," Harry replied. "Out of the darkness into the light—from a desert to an oasis—a kind of heaven, if you like, full of the finest dreams you'll ever have, and you'll have them forever. I think that's where you'll find your Ma and Da, Molly. And if so all that you've told me will be proven to be true. Not that I doubted you for a moment."

How, proven to be true?

"Because the dead are only allowed into that better place according to merit, which means the transition takes some of them a long, long time. Only the good and the innocent go there quickly, while the bad linger on in the dark. And the truly evil ones never get there at all."

Ahhh! She sighed...but then said: *Then tell Oi, Harry, how is it Oi's still here? Were Oi as evil as all that?*

He shrugged, but not negligently, and said, "Perhaps you weren't trying hard enough."

Hard enough? But Oi weren't tryin' at all, at all! Oi didn't even know as how Oi had to try!

"Well, now you do," said the Necroscope. "Just dream a good dream, that's all, and try to will yourself into it. Now that you know the better place is there, it should be easier."

But why haven't others o' the Great Majority told Oi the secret o' it? Molly cried. *Why, Oi might have been gone from here long and long ago!*

"But you see," said Harry, "people don't really understand it or accept it until it happens to them. They might sense that it's there, but if they don't strive for it they must simply wait their turn. And they can't be told of it, can't learn of it from those who have gone before, for they are already out of range and there's no contact with them."

For a moment or two Molly was silent, thoughtful, then said: *No contact with them. Only with ye, eh, Harry?*

"So it would seem," he answered, with another almost apologetic shrug.

But it's really there, this better place, eh?

"Oh, yes."

Then Oi shall strive for it!

"Good!" said Harry.

But for now, she gave a determined nod of her head, *Oi'll finish what Oi started, an' go on trundlin' the old barrow through the dark night streets. If ye'll excuse Oi?*

"Of course," he replied. "For that's the way it is: you'll continue to do in death what you did in life—at least for a little while longer. Goodbye, and good luck, Molly!"

And off she went:
A-live a-live O! A-live a-live O! Cockles an' mussels, alive a-live O!

At the end of his fourth evening in Dublin's fair city, when the shadow of night crept like a great soft mantle over streets broad and narrow, Harry Keogh, Necroscope, lay in his bed and thought of tomorrow morning when he would be moving on.

Of course, with the Möbius route at his disposal he could have moved on at any time he desired. "Even now—*right* now!" he told himself. "At this very minute—if I chose."

As to why he hadn't so chosen: "I *have* enjoyed the break," he muttered to himself. "I've enjoyed Dublin, the accommodation, the food..." And then, with a small shudder, "but no cockles, mussels, or any kind of shellfish! And late last night...I especially enjoyed talking to Molly Malone. But tomorrow morning I'll settle my bill, and moments later I'll be back in Edinburgh. As for Molly—"

At which the real reason he was holding back became obvious...even to Harry himself, who no longer tried to deny it.

It was Molly, of course. She was the reason, and he wondered how she was getting on—wondered if her "striving" had paid off and moved her closer to a transition. And now that it was probably too late, he also wondered how she had looked, sweet Molly Malone, in those long-gone days when she had worked in the city's streets broad and narrow. He could have asked to see her as she remembered herself but hadn't done so in fear of being disappointed. He preferred to "remember" her as he'd always imagined her: a lovely young woman whose sweet slim figure had always seemed oddly incongruous in her fishmonger's street vendor attire.

But yes, it was definitely too late, for while as always the deadspeak ether was full of the faint and various whispers of the Great Majority, the cries that the Necroscope was straining to hear weren't there—

—Or were they?

For fainter than all the other thoughts, complaints,

exclamations of horror and intimations of mortality (these last from the more recently dead, who weren't yet sure of the awful truth,) at long last he was rewarded by the distant, scarcely audible murmur of a deadspeak voice he at last recognized as Molly's. But now, instead of her usually clear but somehow mournful echoing cry—*A-live a-live O! A-live a-live O!*—there was joy, great joy however faint and rapidly fading, reaching his metaphysical mind, but barely, as from a million miles away.

It was there for a moment only, and then gone. And the Necroscope smiled to himself, lay his head on his pillow, and at last slept.

And once again as so often before, he knew who and why he was.

But there was one thing more Harry could do, though he made sure no one but he himself would ever hear the last verse that he added to Molly's song:

> *She died of a fever and no one could save her,*
> *But that isn't the end of sweet Molly Malone!*
> *For she's gone far away, where the gentle folk play,*
> *Living out better days in that sweetest of homes.*
> *A-live a-live O! She's a-live, a-live O!*
> *And there'll ne'er be an end to sweet Molly Malone...*

AUTHOR'S NOTE

Despite exhaustive research, the complete *original* lyrics to Molly Malone have not been found to be copyrighted!

Brian Lumley

THREE SHORT STORIES
IN JUST FIFTY WORDS EACH

One: The Do-It-Yourself Carpenter

The idea was to take some six-by-fours, a handful of nails and a little inspiration, and start a craze to change the entire world. Impossible? But he did it! Blood, sweat and tears played their parts—personal sacrifice, you know? They rewarded him with a crown of thorns.

Two: War of the Worlds

Ron and Mikh, joining forces, went out to explore space. There they found an alien race: weird shapes, sizes...sexes! Outnumbered, the armies of Ron and Mikh bred and bred, finally defeating their diversified foe. Mankind stood no chance against intelligent amoebas whose single strategy was to divide and conquer.

Three: Decreation

Monday. Looking down from on high the astronaut gaped. Where was everyone? On Tuesday the quadrupeds disappeared; Wednesday, the birds and fishes; Thursday saw sun and stars snuffed, the moon magicked away. Then the trees died, and Saturday was Chaos. But the astronaut's guess was right: on Sunday God rested...

FOUR FAVOURITE POEMS
FROM "GHOUL WARNING"

And finally four stories, which, as I wrote them, somehow metamorphosed into poems. It strikes me now that I may well have squandered quite a few a few embryonic short stories that way!

One: CITY OUT OF TIME

Betrayed by dreams I wander weirdling ways,
Beneath the fronds of palms in jungles old
When Earth herself was young and brave and bold.
Where hybrid blooms sway serpentine I gaze
On ruins which no other eyes have seen,
Whose black foundations sink in primal green,
A-crawl with efts of prehistoric days.
Beyond odd-angled ruins ceaseless pound
The waves of frenzied ocean freshly borned,
Which never yet Man's ancestor have spawned,
And here I find strange mysteries profound:
These monoliths of which I stand in awe—
Who built them upon this ancient shore?
And what wild secrets have the ages drowned?
From books in waking worlds I know the name
Of such a city lost in oceans deep,
Where Ancient Ones in unquiet slumbers keep
The lore of dark dimensions and the flame
Of elder magicks burning, 'til a time

When upward from the aeon-silted slime
Vast shapes will come—as once before they came.
Aye, and that fane of evil was R'lyeh,
Where dreaming Cthulhu lies in chains that bind,
Sending his nightmares out to humankind,
Drowning their noble dreams in nameless mire.
And dreaming still I start as from the pile
Snake tentacular arms and in a while—
A *face* that crowns the bulk of Evil's Sirel

Two: A CRY AT NIGHT

That sound—despair, frustration intertwined,
The loneliness of this abode reflected,
Impinging on my being, on my mind—
The crying of my cat, all day neglected.
He sallied forth this morning, still unfed,
To search the nearby wilds for some fair She,
And now, so late, it seems that hunger's led
Old Tom back home that he may now woo me.
My tale can wait—I throw my pen aside—
He howls so strange, perhaps Old Tom is hurt!
A lesson to you, Tom, who can't abide
Beside the hearth but must go out to flirt.
I fling the door wide, laughing—but out there
…It is not Tom who crouches on the stair!

Three: WARHORSE

When the din of the battle was over I found
The mount of a warlord, a-lathered but sound.
His hooves were as red as the ground where he stood,
On a mound of the dead, in a valley of blood.
And he pawed at his master and gave a wild cry,
As if to say: "Lord, this is no place to die!"
But his master was gone and the wound in his head
Spoke of life that was done, of a spirit well fled.
As I caught at his bridle he whinnied and reared,

And baring his teeth stood red-eyed and flat-eared.
Then—great beast that he was—he stood there and cried,
And he laid down beside his old master and died.
If I'm ever a warlord of legendry deed,
Crom grant me love of just such a steed!

Four: **INMATE**

Though you assure me I have dwelled too long
Upon strange things which do not bear recall,
And tell me that the hideous hunting throng
Which seeks my soul does not exist at all,
I say to you that you have never seen
The like of those who haunt my dreams at night,
For then you, too, would soon have fled the scene
Or such a horror, gibbering in fright.
It is not hard for you to say my mind
Is ill and needs to rest and must not dwell
Upon those things which only seek to bind
Me to my own multi-dimensioned hell.
I laugh at you who have not heard the calls
Of those who dwell behind these padded walls!
Your voices, reassuring and warm.
With human kindness brimming in each word,
Decry the things I know that I have heard,
And view my "crazy fancies" with alarm.
The mind (you say) is hard to understand,
With secret, sunken places deep inside,
Where such as I retreat and try to hide
When little things don't go as we had planned.
And patiently you work on me each day,
And pride yourselves when I at last agree,
And nod my bead and say: "Ah, yes—I see!"
But then, at last, when you all go away—
I laugh at you who have not heard the calls
Of those who dwell *behind* these padded walls!

About the Author

Born in County Durham, he joined the British Army's Royal Military Police and wrote stories in his spare time before retiring with the rank of Warrant Officer Class 2 in 1980 and becoming a professional writer.

In the 1970s he added to H. P. Lovecraft's Cthulhu Mythos cycle of stories, including several tales and a novel featuring the character Titus Crow. Several of his early books were published by Arkham House. Other stories pastiched Lovecraft's Dream Cycle but featured Lumley's original characters David Hero and Eldin the Wanderer. Lumley once explained the difference between his Cthulhu Mythos characters and Lovecraft's: "My guys fight back. Also, they like to have a laugh along the way."

Later works included the Necroscope® series of novels, which produced spin-off series such as the Vampire World Trilogy, The Lost Years parts 1 and 2, and the E-Branch trilogy. The central protagonist of the earlier Necroscope® novels appears in the anthology Harry Keogh and Other Weird Heroes. The latest entry in the Necroscope saga is The Möbius Murders. Lumley served as president of the Horror Writers Association from 1996 to 1997. In March 2010, Lumley was awarded Lifetime Achievement Award of the Horror Writers Association. He also received a World Fantasy Award for Lifetime Achievement in 2010.

Bibliography

Psychomech Trilogy
Psychomech
Psychosphere
Psychamok

Necroscope® Series
Necroscope
Necroscope II: Wamphyri!
Necroscope III: The Source
Necroscope IV: Deadspeak
Necroscope V: Deadspawn
Vampire World I: Blood Brothers
Vampire World II: The Last Aerie
Vampire World III: Bloodwars
Necroscope: The Lost Years, Volume I
Necroscope: The Lost Years, Volume II
Necroscope: Invaders
Necroscope: Defilers
Necroscope: Avengers
Harry Keogh: Necroscope & Other Weird Heroes
Necroscope: The Touch
Necroscope: The Möbius Murders

Dreamland Series
Hero of Dreams
Ship of Dreams
Mad Moon of Dreams
Iced on Aran

Curious about other Crossroad Press books?
Stop by our site:
http://store.crossroadpress.com
We offer quality writing
in digital, audio, and print formats.

Printed in Great Britain
by Amazon

41724228R00108